"It occurred to me," he said gravely,
"that we haven't made love in three days."

A small, slow smile curved on her lips. "We aren't a wee bit bored with this gathering, are we, Mr. Hamilton?" she murmured.

"We have done our duty, Mrs. Hamilton. If you'll remember correctly, we had some very different plans for these three days in Chicago. I've noticed it before, lady. You are a very, very good sport."

"I am," she agreed impishly, "very, very good."

"And I think it's time to skip out and cut up a little. Maybe we'll just walk for a while."

She knew damn well he wanted her alone, where the door was locked against interruptions.

"Walking is what you have in mind, is it?"

"For starters."

With a lazy grin, he claimed her wrist, not wasting any more time...

Jeanne Grant *is a native of Michigan, where she and her husband own cherry and peach orchards, and also grow strawberries. In addition to raising two children, she has worked as a teacher, counselor, and personnel manager. Jeanne began writing at age ten. She's an avid reader as well, and says, "I don't think anything will ever beat a good love story"*

Dear Reader:

More than one year ago, at a time when romance readers were asking for "something different," we took a bold step in romance publishing by launching an innovative new series of books about married love: TO HAVE AND TO HOLD.

Since then, TO HAVE AND TO HOLD has developed a faithful following of enthusiastic readers. We're still delighted to receive your letters—which come from teenagers, grandmothers, and women of every age in between, both married and single. All of you have one quality in common—you believe that love and romance exist beyond the "happily ever after" endings of more conventional stories.

This month we bring you *Conquer the Memories* by our very popular Jeanne Grant. Jennifer Rose also returns with *Pennies From Heaven*. And Kate Nevins, whom some of you know as the author of several SECOND CHANCE AT LOVE romances, has written her first TO HAVE AND TO HOLD, *Memory and Desire*, coming in January. Be sure, too, not to overlook the "newcomers" you'll continue to see in TO HAVE AND TO HOLD. This month Joan Darling debuts with *Tyler's Folly*, a unique, witty story that made me laugh out loud. We're proud to bring these wonderfully talented writers to you!

Warmest wishes,

Ellen Edwards

Ellen Edwards, Senior Editor
TO HAVE AND TO HOLD
The Berkley Publishing Group
200 Madison Avenue
New York, N.Y. 10016

CONQUER
THE MEMORIES

JEANNE
GRANT

SECOND CHANCE AT LOVE
BOOK

Other books by *Jeanne Grant*

CONQUER THE MEMORIES

First edition published December 1984

First printing

"Second Chance at Love," the butterfly emblem, and "To Have and to Hold" are trademarks belonging to Jove Publications, Inc.

Printed in the United States of America

To Have and to Hold books are published by
The Berkley Publishing Group
200 Madison Avenue, New York, NY 10016

CONQUER
THE MEMORIES

1

"I'M TELLING YOU, Craig, you could make it in politics. Energy is still the public's favorite subject, particularly since the latest crisis in the Middle East. With the handle you've got on oil shale..."

"I hear you, sir." Above the elderly ex-senator's shoulder, Craig Hamilton spotted his wife. For an instant, all he could see was a single splash of bright emerald through a zigzag path of dark business suits and broad shoulders. That particular shade of green was *not* his favorite color. "You'll like the dress when you see it on," Sonia had told him.

Actually, he didn't. As he got a better view of Sonia, Craig decided that the neck of the dress annoyed him— there wasn't any. Sonia had a beautiful throat, long and white, her delicate collarbones framing the hollow that always pulsed when she was excited. So vulnerable, that ivory flesh. And just above the silky green fabric, anyone could see the rise of her breasts.

She laughed suddenly, her springy black curls dancing around her cheeks. Three men from the press surrounded her, but Craig could still catch the sparkle of her animated aquamarine eyes from two dozen feet away.

Now that he thought about it, the whole dress annoyed him. The gown was just a little too much like a game of show-and-tell. The way the sneaky little slit showed off her legs every time she took a step, for instance. And no, not another soul in the room could conceivably tell from the design of the dress that she was braless, but

1

Craig knew. He happened to have . . . been there when she was dressing.

"You've got the money," former senator Rafe Bradford continued, "and, more important, you've got the power. People *listen* to you, Craig. Why, in my day, I'd have sold my soul to get the kind of public support you already have."

Craig snagged a glass of champagne for the older man from a passing waiter. He didn't bother to contradict anything Bradford said, although privately Craig knew he'd prefer digging ditches to a political career any day. But the ex-senator had once been a friend of his family's, and the man was old and lonely.

"Everyone in this room knows you were the principal adviser to the Senate subcommittee on shale oil . . ."

The sash on that damn dress drew in her waist, accenting its tiny proportions. And Sonia had a way with her eyes that captivated everyone, including the press. Craig's mouth twitched as he watched her effortlessly charm Andrew Roth, the most cynical of national news commentators. Roth had called this national conference defining the new relationship between energy and ecology a scam; he claimed the "relationship" was a contradiction in terms and always would be. Sonia was setting him straight. Roth's bald head was bobbing up and down . . .

"Not that it's any of my business, but you have that little ranch—and people do love a man with a feeling for the land. A self-made man. Oil shale always had a bad press until you tackled it with that new extraction process of yours. We're all hungry for a way to get out of our dependency on foreign oil, as long as it's not at our own expense. And you could *use* that expertise of yours to help us do just that, son."

The four long tables covered with white linen where the conference dinner had been served stood empty now. The featured event of the evening had been Craig's keynote speech. But this type of gathering didn't wear well on him. Not that he wasn't committed to the subject matter. Having found an ecologically acceptable method of extracting oil from shale, he was more than willing to share his ideas, if not his trade secrets. The three-day conference had been well attended by political figures and bankers and oil people, and that pleased him, too. The purpose of the gathering was to draw members of opposing factions together—but he hadn't anticipated the political machinations that were going on. Financial games, power plays, people using the conference to serve their own ends... manipulation of that sort made him grit his teeth.

Sonia would have chided him for his characteristic lack of patience, if she'd seen him. At the moment, she was giving a hug and kiss to Warren Radley, a senator who could use his strong influence to persuade the government to fund shale-oil research. Warren's eyes soulfully followed the sway of Sonia's emerald hips as she wandered away from him. Next, Sonia offered a quick, chilly handshake to Barker Cole, an oil man notorious for raping the land. She didn't like him. Cole was certainly the more prominent of the two men, but that cut no ice with Sonia. She liked Warren because he was sensitive about being only five feet four and because he raised Irish setters. Cole, she'd told Craig often enough, could sink himself into the nearest pit.

"Use of power, son. Use of power is everything!" Rafe Bradford exhorted. But Craig's thoughts were still on his wife.

A hand whipped around Sonia's waist, dragging her close for a friendly peck. Her aquamarine eyes turned the identical shade of emerald of her dress. Sonia was made on affectionate lines, and affection offered freely was one thing; a stolen touch was another. She treated Ferrel Romnay to a stare that would have frozen Popsicles on a ninety-degree day, and to hell with Romnay's banking influence.

Craig did his best to smother a grin, as well as to

swallow the urge to turn the man's nose inside out. Sonia could take care of herself. She'd told him so a thousand times.

Craig controlled an inner wince as John Smith and his wife crossed Sonia's path. Perhaps they would discuss the weather? But no, Sonia had taken Ferona Smith's March for Clean Air as a personal attack on Craig. Sonia had a low tolerance for professional do-gooders who took up causes without doing their homework on them first. As she warmed up to the subject, her skin took on the flush of coral, and her chin tilted just that little bit upward.

His wife, Craig thought idly, certainly wasn't shy. She undoubtedly knew more of the people at the conference than he did—because of her bubbly friendliness in most instances. She had to be one of the most spectacularly beautiful women . . .

"Hamilton?"

Craig's eyes pivoted directly back to the former senator's. "I'm sorry. Sir?"

"You've been kind to listen," the older man said gruffly, and motioned in Sonia's direction with a sparkle of humor in his tired gray eyes. "Perhaps, though, you ought to go over there and rescue your better half?"

"Perhaps," Craig agreed gravely, "that would be wise."

It wasn't so easy to travel the twenty-five feet to Sonia's side. For a man who eighteen years earlier had been orphaned with no property save a bankrupt ranch in an obscure corner of Wyoming, he'd certainly come a long way; there was no counting the number of people who went out of their way to talk with him now. Having made his mark in Cold Creek—a town few people here had even heard of—Craig was still occasionally amused that anyone from Washington should go to such trouble to seek him out at this gathering. He was a private man, without the slightest interest in earning public acclaim. Actually, the only thing on his mind at the moment was collecting Sonia and getting the hell out of here.

* * *

Some sixth sense told Sonia that Craig was approaching. It was strange, but somehow she had only to intuit his proximity and her every feminine instinct was aroused. For the hundredth time, she thought idly that it was really very difficult not to be proud of him, even if she did have to bully him into coming here.

She didn't have to spot him to know the look of him, wending his way through the crowd, a boyish shock of brown hair on his forehead, a disgracefully all-American smile catching every woman's eye. He moved in lithe, lazy motions, with an easy sensuality that never betrayed tension. Tell me your secrets, said those brilliant blue eyes. If one looked closely enough, one could see the crow's-feet around those eyes, and the experience and character in his strong features that bespoke his thirty-five years. He was five feet ten; he carried himself like a man of six eleven. *Naturally,* people cornered him to talk. People envied his self-assurance, his vitality . . .

Sonia wasn't a bit prejudiced.

Well, a little, perhaps. Her husband had a few glaring faults. She generally treated those carefully. For instance, since she planned to be married to him for all of her next thousand lives, she figured she still had plenty of time to convince him that it was okay to take an occasional laurel for who he was and what he'd already done with his life.

In the meantime, she'd been watching him. He liked being in Chicago about as much as he'd liked spending six months in Washington last year—which was not at all. Cities turned him off. He hadn't let it show, however, during his talks at the conference and the speech tonight. And after dinner, when a dozen prominent men were all but flag-waving to get his attention, he'd offered his time to Bradford, such a lonely old man these days.

Long firm fingers closed on her waist from behind, and Sonia glanced up with a private smile for her husband, his mere closeness making her eyes light up like

Fourth of July sparklers. The half-frown on his forehead was there and gone before another soul could have noticed. Sonia, immediately perceptive, ended the argument with Ferona as Craig's arm circled her shoulders.

"What's wrong?" she murmured as she found herself inexorably led away from the crowd. Just outside the hotel's banquet room was a darkly paneled hallway filled with coat racks and all but empty of people.

"It occurred to me . . ." Craig paused as someone unexpectedly entered the hallway and stopped to exchange a word or two. When they were alone again, he wrapped both his arms around Sonia's shoulders and enclosed them both immediately in their own private cocoon. In Sonia's line of vision were Craig's stiffly starched white shirt, his spring-weight black suit jacket, the shock of brown hair on his forehead, and those Paul Newman blues of his. No one else. Nothing else. "It occurred to me," he repeated gravely, "that we haven't made love in nearly three days."

She stared at him blankly before a small, slow smile curved mischievously on her lips. "We aren't a wee bit bored with this gathering, are we, Mr. Hamilton?" she murmured.

"We have done our duty, Mrs. Hamilton."

She shook her head. "There's still a line of people in there wanting to talk to you when they get the chance, and you know it."

"You talked to all of them. I don't need to."

"They're expecting—"

He shook his head. "If you'll remember correctly, Mrs. Hamilton, we had some very different plans for these three days in Chicago. A little shopping, a little time alone together; you wanted to see that art fair. Instead, I haven't even had breakfast alone with you, and you've been asleep long before I could escape the crowd at night. I've noticed it before, lady. You are a very, very good sport."

"I am," she agreed impishly, "very, very good."

"And I think it's time to skip out and cut up a little."

"Oh?"

Craig's thumb idly traced her cheekbone. A very high, delicate cheekbone. He was tremendously fond of those bones. And those incredible deep-set green-blue eyes, always so full of emotion, so sensitive to his every mood. She had a tiny black beauty mark at the nape of her neck and wore her curly black hair just long enough to conceal it. He loved that mark, too. And the legs that could have been a dancer's . . . she was all leg, he told her often. She regularly apologized for being so misshapen.

She was wearing her cat's smile at the moment, her eyes unspeakably demure beneath a fringe of thick, dark lashes. She knew damn well that in his eyes she was shaped perfectly. And that he was tired of people and wanted her alone, where the phone was off the hook and the door was locked against interruptions.

"First, we're going to hear some music," he told her huskily. "And then maybe we'll just walk for a while."

"Walking is what you have in mind, is it?"

"For starters."

Sonia made a big business out of straightening his tie. Scarlet and black striped, very conservative. So was his starched white shirt. Beneath that shirt his heart was beating at a very unconservative rate—and it continued to accelerate the longer her hands lingered at his throat, the longer her breast brushed just lightly against his arm. Her husband responded like quicksilver. Disgraceful, after being married four years. She reached up to brush back that wayward shock of light brown hair that had fallen over his forehead. The gesture was frankly proprietary. One of these days she was going to get him out of those starched white shirts if it killed her. She would not insist on pastels; that would be a hopeless mismatch with his character, but a simple masculine stripe wouldn't hurt him. "It was an honor to be invited, and I really think you should be busy in there—"

"Your mother always says that busy hands are happy

hands," Craig agreed. "Mine are itching at this moment
to get very busy, Mrs. Hamilton."

"There's just no talking to you," she informed him.

With a lazy grin, he claimed her wrist, not wasting
any more time. They quickly said the necessary good-byes
to the people Craig honestly cared for and respected, and
then made their escape.

The lobby of the hotel was swarming with people;
through a revolving glass door they were suddenly set
free in Chicago at night. A late spring breeze whispered
off nearby Lake Michigan. At eleven o'clock, Chicago's
night life was just getting started. Sequins and silks flashed
by in passing car windows, and Sonia paused for a moment, seeing the promise of excitement in the gleam of
neon lights. She no more valued big-city pollution than
Craig did; they both loved their ranch at Cold Creek with
its backdrop of mountains. Tonight, though, Chicago had
its own special appeal. The air actually smelled fresh,
with a lingering hint of spring. Or perhaps she was just
susceptible to becoming intoxicated at the idea of escaping responsibilities and people and smoke-filled rooms.

"We'll go back to our hotel and change clothes," Craig
directed as they crossed the six-lane street to where their
rented car was parked. "Put on something comfortable.
We'll go out and just fool around for an hour or two."

"And then come back to get a good eight hours of
sleep," Sonia said demurely.

"Or its equivalent."

"I was never very good at math. What is the *equivalent*
of eight hours of sleep?" Sonia wondered aloud.

"I may," Craig remarked, "develop a fetish for spank-
ing. Soon." She slipped into the car. Automatically, his
thumb punched down the lock button before he closed
her door. Just as automatically, when he got in on his
side his arm immediately strapped her in at shoulder and
waist; then, when he had her pinned like a moth, he
proceeded to kiss her thoroughly. As he released her and
started the engine, Sonia thought idly that Craig's pro-

tectiveness was instinctive, something he probably wasn't even aware of. She was.

The moment they pulled out onto the street, a small dark blue car appeared right behind them. Sonia knew Craig saw it, because he checked the rearview mirror. "Shadow" had come with the conference, and their unasked-for bodyguard thoroughly irritated her.

Emotions ran high on anything remotely connected to energy and the Middle East; she knew that, just as she knew Craig had joined the ranks of wealthy and influential men in the last few years. The conference organizers routinely provided protection for important participants, but Sonia knew Craig wouldn't have put up with Shadow if she hadn't been along.

When they'd been in Washington, she'd had more than a moment or two of worry when she realized how volatile certain groups could be. Mention oil and the ecologists cocked their panic guns at the same time that people with vested interests in fossil fuels got touchy. So a little prudence was called for, but Sonia certainly had no intention of living her life in a perpetual state of paranoia. She resented Shadow as she resented toothaches, and glancing back at their tail, she felt a damper clamp down on her ebullient mood.

"The conference is over. We don't have to have him with us if we're just going out for a few hours, do we?" she pleaded.

For a moment, she thought Craig hadn't heard her. His foot pressed down on the accelerator as the light turned green. He adjusted the car's ventilation to let in some fresh air, loosened his tie, and weaved promptly around a driver who was straddling two lanes.

"Of course we don't," he said finally.

And immediately regretted that decision. He knew Sonia hated their tail, and he knew she'd guessed that Stoner was there primarily to protect her. Craig would never have put up with Stoner for himself alone, regardless of the knife someone had tried to poke at him

in Sheridan, Wyoming, two years before. Sonia didn't
know about that, and never would. At the time, he'd
hadn't known whether his attacker was after his wallet
or angry over his work with shale oil. It didn't matter.
Sonia did.

He couldn't stand the thought of something happening
to her.

For the last three days, though, whenever he spotted
Stoner's car in his rearview mirror, he felt like a preten-
tious fool. He might have a little money, and for a short
while maybe he was in a modest limelight. He was still
just a man, and a man who'd known how to defend
himself from the time he was nine.

In protecting Sonia, however, it was unlike him to let
his better judgment be swayed by impulse. He didn't like
big cities and knew the conference had received national
publicity, so he had no regrets about taking on Stoner—
but dammit, at the moment he just wanted to be with his
wife. He wanted the freedom to make her laugh, to talk
nonsense, and simply *play* without an audience. To make
love later, yes, but first to cherish a few stolen hours of
privacy with her. It wasn't as though Stoner had spent
the last three days staring at them, but the few minutes
they'd had alone together just hadn't been enough.

After he parked the car in the hotel garage, Craig
stalked back to have a word with the other man. Sonia
waited by the car until he returned. "What'd you say to
him?" she asked.

"That we were retiring for the night."

Her chuckle was delighted; her bright eyes were
sparkling. "So we get to escape from the big bad wolf?"

"Sonia—"

"Oh, Lord, what if he decides to read the paper in the
lobby? We'd better sneak down to the back door."

He shook his head ruefully, loving her bubble of excitement, knowing exactly how much they both valued
their privacy. "You've been reading too many spy stories. But if we're going to take off like thieves in the

night, we'd better change clothes." His finger just touched
her nose. "Think you could manage to look mousy and
inconspicuous for a little while?"

"I'll fade right into the shadows," Sonia promised.
Craig had so many responsibilities, particularly this last
year, that she was delighted to see him shed those cares
in favor of sheer mischievous fun. By the time they
reached the twelfth floor, he was laughing.

He stabbed the key in the lock, opened the door to
their room, and relocked it after they entered. "Strip,"
he ordered promptly.

"Oh, Lord. Is this one of those your-virtue-or-your-
money capers?"

"You have to be joking," Craig retorted. "I've never
seen you travel with more than thirty-seven cents in your
pocket. Skin is all I'm interested in, lady."

She slipped out of her emerald dress and tossed it to
him; he tossed her his jacket. They hung up each other's
clothes, laughing. Watching her play half naked, Craig
forgot ninety percent of his good intentions, particularly
once they'd exchanged his shirt and her coral satin half
slip. Sonia *was* all leg. Perfect legs, firm, slim thighs
and spectacular calves, her fanny close to irresisti-
ble . . . and deliberately swaying in his direction, he noticed.

Her small, pert breasts were the same ivory color as
her complexion, the rosy nipples sassily pointed up at
him. And after knowing her for almost five years and
being married for better than four, Craig's reaction to
the look of her was as instantly, blatantly physical as
when he'd first met her.

Sonia's original reaction to Craig had been markedly
different. Her mother, who was generally inclined to pick
up loners around the holidays, had been the one who'd
found him and dragged him home for Thanksgiving. At
the time, Sonia wasn't part of the ranching community
anymore; for the past few years, she'd had an apartment
in Boulder and was working as a buyer for a women's

boutique there. She had a distinctly different definition
of "innocent loner" than her mother did. Craig didn't
qualify. Nor had he acquired that considerable expertise
of his anywhere near an oil field. Sonia knew trouble
when she saw it, and had every intention of spending
that particular Thanksgiving in the kitchen. It didn't quite
work out that way.

Though flamboyant in dress and gregarious with people, at twenty-five Sonia still had been reserved at the
thought of real intimacy. Her mother used to tell her that
she'd already worked through more men than the county
had fence posts, but appearances were deceiving. Sonia
appreciated a well-cast line, but she was not so naive as
to let herself be taken in by one. When she'd met Craig,
she could have fit her previous sexual experience in a
teacup.

But he'd certainly taken care of that problem since,
she thought wickedly. Poor man, now he suffered the
consequences. The longer she wandered around bare-
topped, the more trouble he was having getting into his
jeans. Her own denims snapped, but just, designed to fit
her shapely bottom snugly, molding the legs Craig was
so fond of. She donned a red silk blouse without bra,
left a button or two open, and vigorously took a brush
to her curls... which, actually, never helped her stubborn hairstyle anyway. A quick slash of lipstick and a
pair of elegant walking boots, and she turned around
with a sassy grin.

"Inconspicuous enough?" she demanded.

He shook his head in sheer despair.

"What's wrong?"

He was afraid if he gave her the list they would never
leave the hotel room. His kitten looked ready to prowl,
and instinctively he wanted to set off the first purrs. In
the meantime, she could have worn a sign on her smile
that said VULNERABLE as far as walking Chicago's streets
at night went. "For starters, the opal," he began.

She glanced at the mirror. She never took off the black

opal that dangled from a gold chain on her neck; he'd given it to her on their honeymoon. The oval stone was a myriad of green-blues that matched her eyes, just as its onyx setting matched her hair. Only reluctantly did Sonia tie a scarlet and white scarf at her throat to cover it. "Better?" she questioned, already knowing his opinion.

Her husband didn't approve of the fit of her jeans any more than he approved of the scarlet blouse...or the emerald dress she'd worn earlier. He approved of her naked, preferably locked in a room alone with him.

Deep inside, Craig harbored a dreadfully medieval male protectiveness and jealousy. Sonia adored him all the more because of it. It took a very special kind of man to control those intense feelings and encourage his lady to live her own life in her own way, not just follow along in his shadow. It was tough for a strong, dominant man to make a marriage of equals; Sonia was well aware that Craig worked at it.

It was absolutely necessary to give him a long, lingering kiss before they headed out into the hall, ready and eager for a few hours of privacy together in a town of some three million people. That they would find it, neither had any doubt. They only needed each other.

2

LAKE MICHIGAN LAY black and smooth, its still surface glazed with stars. At two in the morning, the city's traffic was finally settling down. They might almost have been home, Sonia reflected—the park was that serene and restful. Huge shade trees nestled the two of them in privacy, and the smell of new green leaves and damp, sweet grass was intoxicating, so fresh with new life that it was impossible to get enough of the scent of it. Sonia simply inhaled, loving all the aromas of spring.

"Did you like the music?" Craig murmured.

"Mmm." She'd loved the nightclub and the music. And the three glasses of champagne. And being alone with her husband. And now, that special quiet of an early, early morning in late May.

Waves of contentment just kept coming. Everything felt special—the dew-drenched grass beneath her walking boots, the feel of the cool, silky blouse against her bare skin, the touch of a breeze fingering through her hair. Happiness flooded through her like a roller coaster; the rush just wouldn't stop. Sonia felt high like rainbows—a phrase in her head that made no particular sense. She told it to Craig. "Explain it to me," she suggested whimsically.

Always, her husband had had an uncanny understanding of even her most obscure thoughts. He tugged her into the shadow of a sheltering maple, leaned back against the bark, and experimented with explaining "high like rainbows."

14

He captured the basic idea when his lips whispered across her temples, then her nose, then her cheeks. He caught even more of the concept when his fingers languidly sifted through her hair. As he leaned back against the tree, his legs were slightly parted, encouraging her to fit just so in that inviting spread of his thighs.

She forgot all about rainbows. His lips touched base with hers, and neither wanted to let go. Through his dark sweatshirt, through her thin silk blouse, she could feel her breasts suddenly aching, rubbing against him, and his heartbeat throbbed in response.

Her lips parted and closed on the lower curve of his, her kisses deliberately tempting, invitingly feminine. She courted the dramatic response of his body . . . the low groan from the back of his throat as he gathered her closer, the tightening of his thighs, the way his arms turned possessive. It would have been so easy to have rushed into bed earlier. Those few hours alone together and all the laughter they had shared made the waiting so much sweeter, like a long, lazy seduction that refused to end. They were still miles from their hotel, and her teasing was the more provocative because of it. She wanted this night to last forever . . .

From somewhere in the distance she heard a vague sound. The lovers they'd passed on the way in? No matter—she and Craig were hidden in shadows. His tongue stole between her lips and started a slow, gradual exploration—the inside of her cheek, the back of her teeth, the roof of her mouth.

Her hands splayed, running down his sides to his hips. Her fingertips could just reach the middle of his thighs, hard thighs encased in rough denim. Her fingers were enjoying the long, leisurely walk up again, stealing under his sweatshirt, needing the feel of his bare skin. When the flat of her palms covered his taut male breasts, she could feel his temperature rise three degrees. He had a delightfully feverish look in his eyes . . .

"It's time to go home," he said gruffly.

"Yes."

He buried his face in her throat, pulling her even closer to himself. Her skin was so supple, so soft; she smelled so sweetly of Sonia. The need to possess her had become a driving hunger. "When we get back," he whispered to her, "I'm going to take off your blouse, Sonia. Then your jeans. I'm going to place you on the bed..."

She shivered, a delicious wave of pure sensual anticipation sensitizing every nerve ending of her skin.

"I'm going to turn you over on your stomach," he whispered, his lips very close to her ear. Then they nestled in her hair and finally in the hollow of her shoulder. "I'm going to kiss the backs of your knees, then the length of your spine, then that small fanny of yours. Then up to that tiny birthmark at the nape of your neck..."

"Craig—"

"Then I'm going to turn you over and just look at you. Just...watch you. The way your breasts swell, the way they ache with heat...I can feel it. I can feel them change in the palm of my hand. I can feel it when you want me..."

Her conservative, civilized businessman had turned into a pirate from another century. Long, drugging kisses backed up all the promise in his words, inflaming Sonia with a wild, haunting recklessness as she matched kiss for kiss, caress for caress.

"Take me home," she murmured pleadingly.

The teasing had been fun, the park romantic, the nightclub wonderful... and she'd always loved champagne, drank it as if it were soda pop. But it was sharing all these things with Craig that made them pleasures. Being with him was what mattered; the rest was just frosting on the cake. And she was no longer interested in frosting.

He kissed her again, and then, unsmiling, drew back, gently smoothing her hair before tucking her into the hollow of his shoulder.

They were looking at each other as they started walking. The same message was in both of their expressions. Stark need, the lushness of anticipation, and the irrepressible desire they both had to laugh at their own mutual craziness at wanting each other too damn much for married people in a public park. Craig, a man who never lost control, and Sonia, the lady who was once so sure that inhibitions and intimacy were a matched set . . . The corner of his mouth suddenly twitched, and she stood on tiptoe to kiss him hard.

"You think you can behave yourself long enough to get back to the hotel?" he whispered.

She shook her head, laughing. "Now, don't go shifting the blame. I was just standing here, being a meek little submissive wife, tolerating my . . . er . . . conjugal responsibilities."

"Tolerating, were you?"

"Good Lord, you didn't think I was turned on?"

His arm tightened around her shoulder while hers wrapped around his waist. There was one fleeting moment when her heart felt full, when the lush brilliance of happiness seemed so tangible she could embrace it . . .

Then nightmare.

Talons clawed her arms, ripping her away from Craig. Shock registered before fear, until an alcohol-crazed pair of eyes loomed in front of her face, leering and laughing. Sonia staggered back, but not fast enough. The man snatched her again, his fingers biting into her arms, dragging her farther away from Craig, farther into the black shadows of trees, slamming her spine into rough bark.

"Craig!"

Her desperate cry came out more whisper than scream. Terror knotted her throat, so instantaneous and bone-chilling that her mind could not grasp what was happening. That man with the terrifying light eyes . . . but he wasn't alone. "Now you just shut up and take it easy, lady," he hissed to her.

Through a frantic blur, she saw three more men surrounding Craig, and yet another standing behind her tor-

mentor. Horror bubbled over. They were all young and
filthy and reeking of liquor, their eyes all similarly glazed.
The one who'd taken her on was the worst, with his long,
stringy blond hair and acid smile... *evil,* her mind hissed.
She tried to lurch up and felt the heel of his hand slam
into her chest.

"Sonia! Run—!"

Through the tangle of limbs, she caught Craig's eyes;
for an instant he looked insane with panic for her. His
shouted curse brought the pack on him. She heard the
terrible sound of fist connecting with bone, and desperately tried to run to him. Her arm was wrenched from
its socket, bent back and behind her, and she was forced
to stumble into the blond man's chest.

"Let her *go,* you—"

Pain stabbed her shoulder as the blond twisted her
arm yet more tightly, cursing. "Keep him *quiet,* I said!"
Craig was being pulled to his feet, two men holding his
arms. One was trying to rifle through his pockets. Craig
kicked out, and there was a confused rush of motion as
he tried to wrench free from his captors. *"Let her go,
you—"* he bellowed again.

A fist connected with his face.

Sonia screamed. Before the sound was halfway from
her mouth, a filthy hand clamped over it, and her arm
was again yanked so roughly that she knew the blond
man was more than willing to break it. She cringed—
inside, outside, all over.

"Fifty bucks," one of Craig's tormentors called out
disgustedly to the man who was holding her.

"What the hell. Get his watch."

"Sonia—"

The blond laughed. The sound made Sonia swallow
with revulsion. "The man sure don't seem to like it much
when we touch his lady, now, does he? *Hold* him, I told
you," he snapped roughly to the others. His voice changed
from command to insinuating drawl. "Maybe the lady's
got a little something of value."

A flush of nausea heated Sonia's face as rough fingers tried to burrow into the pockets of her jeans. She carried no purse; there had been no need to bring one. In the first pocket, all the blond found was a quarter, and for one insane instant Sonia felt the hysterical urge to laugh. Never go anywhere without a coin to make a phone call in an emergency, her mother had told her a thousand times. Sonia wasn't aware she'd never broken the habit.

The blond kept glancing at Craig as he checked the other three pockets. "Man, look at him go," he chortled to the others. God, stay still, she wanted to beg Craig; stay *still,* they just want money. But her husband hadn't stopped struggling from the instant he'd seen the blond grab her.

One rough hand dug into her waist; the other again wrenched her arm behind her until tears blinded her eyes. Nausea clogged her throat; the terror was so acute she was losing her breath, sobbing without even being aware of it. So dark, so black a night, and the smile on the stringy blond's face. . . . He wanted to hurt . . . someone. He was angry they didn't have more money, and he was crazy and he was loaded to the gills.

His free hand crept over her stomach. "Hey, man, she keep anything worth hiding in her blouse?"

He was talking to Craig.

"Don't," Sonia whispered desperately. "Please. *Please . . .*"

The next second took years. That filthy hand deliberately crawled slowly up from her waist. She saw Craig's eyes just those few yards distant from her, insane with rage, brilliant with fury. . . . *No!* her mind screamed to him. *No, Craig, don't!* Don't . . . but before the hand could touch her breast, Craig had broken free from the others and launched himself at the blond.

"Get him!"

A keening moan escaped from Sonia's throat. In a tangle of limbs and fists, Craig was buried beneath the other three. The blond laughed, and Sonia felt terror for herself shoved aside in her brain, an insidious horror taking its place. They were going to kill Craig. She could already see the wet, shiny red liquid on his face. Blood. If some instinct of self-preservation had kept her still before, that instinct died, replaced by another. Desperately, she began to kick the blond; her nails became deadly claws; her teeth snapped at the arm of her tormentor like the fangs of a wounded animal. He grunted, his arms loosening long enough for her to jerk free.

For an instant. She didn't make it to Craig's side. Her face connected with the damp, hard earth, the breath knocked out of her, as the blond tackled her and tossed her hard and flat on the ground. Then he flipped her on her back. Her scarf had disappeared; her opal must have glinted in the moonlight, because she felt the chain being ripped off, slicing a quick, sharp pain at her neck.

"Hell. Split," the leader ordered. "They haven't got a damn thing worth all this hassle anyway."

Like creatures of the night, they took off at a dead run, silent, part of the shadows, and then gone, disappearing as if they had never been. Only one sound pierced the lonely night, the choking whimpers that came out of Sonia's throat, sobs very close to hysteria.

Soaked from the dew-drenched grass, she was freezing, shaking like a mad thing. Sharp, darting pains shot up the arm the blond mugger had wrenched so badly. She *had* to move, *had* to get to Craig, yet nausea still gripped her, and she felt a terrible need to curl up in a ball, to hide. Human beings—they were actually human beings, she thought dazedly. She knew violence only as a statistic in the newspapers—it had never touched her life before.

Tears streaming from her eyes, Sonia jerked herself up to a sitting position. A razor-sharp pain promptly sliced through the back of her head, and an unexpected dizziness overwhelmed her with potent waves of nausea. Her shoulder. . . . She saw Craig lying not five feet from her and forgot her own pain. He was still. There was blood on his face and his legs were sprawled and his skin looked ghost-gray in the moonlight. Damn her tears! She couldn't see through the blur...

Stumbling to her feet, she staggered over to her husband and knelt down, roughly brushing her eyes with the sleeve of her blouse, refusing to let any more tears fall. They didn't. She no longer had time for them.

She put her ear to Craig's chest and her hand on the pulse in his wrist at the same time. That terrible knot loosened its hold on her heart. He was alive. But he was so terrifyingly still....His heartbeat seemed shallow, unsteady. Gently probing with her fingers, Sonia found a swelling mound at the back of his head. The blood on his face was from his nose—had they broken it? He made a low, guttural sound when her fingers gently tested his ribs, then a small spot beneath them. The bastards! The total bastards...

"Craig?"

But his eyelids didn't even flutter. Frantically, she glanced around. Neither blankets nor bandages miraculously appeared. There was no one, not a hint of sound indicating another person might be near. Well, she was *not* going to leave him. Nothing could make her leave him; she *couldn't* leave him...any more than she could continue to let him lie there motionless on the damp, wet grass, unconscious.

"Craig?" Gentle fingers smoothed the hair back from his forehead, gentle, calm fingers. Reassuring. "You're going to be fine. I won't be gone a minute. Just long enough to get help. You'll be fine, darling..."

She touched him one more time before she forced herself to stand up. A thousand years ago she'd learned first-aid skills. Too long. Were the feet supposed to be raised for shock? For concussion? Could she do him harm if she tried to drag him?...Dammit, she couldn't *possibly* leave him like this.

Her heart pounding in her chest, she took off at a dead run, stumbling over the invisible rises and falls in the dark night-shrouded grass. The peaceful park had become a hell for her, with trees looming like menacing ghosts, the silence and darkness ominous and terrifying. Across open lawn, under trees, over paved walkways, she dashed—all of it seemed endless. Unconsciously, she held her hurt arm as she raced, and she kept the pace until her side ached so badly she could hardly breathe. At last she reached the long boulevard that led to Chicago's business loop. A single car passed and then another. If they saw her, they didn't slow down.

Finally, on the other side of the street, she saw a yellow taxi let someone out, and she fled across the shiny black asphalt, mindless of any other traffic that could have been coming. Gasping, she raced in front of the cab before the driver could take off again.

"You've *got* to help me—"

The tall black cab driver seemed startled, and for an instant Sonia realized how odd she must look—filthy and grass-stained and wild-eyed and running out from the middle of nowhere.

"*Help* me. You've got to help me. My husband is hurt—he's lying out there—" She motioned frantically to the dark shadows of the park.

"Look, lady—"

"For *godsake*—"

Wary black eyes pierced hers. "Like take it easy, okay? You want me to call a cop, is that it?"

"An ambulance. No . . ." She ran a frantic hand through her hair. "I want an ambulance, but I need a blanket *now*. Or a jacket or sweater. *Anything*. Couldn't you come? You're big enough. . . . The thing is, I can't move him. He's lying in the grass . . ."

She could read *forget it* in his eyes. The man was street smart, not necessarily unkind. How did he know she wasn't trying to lead him to some setup where *he* might get mugged? She could read his mind in that instant, and couldn't blame him.

She couldn't blame him, but frustration bubbled over

like an insane rage she couldn't control. She slammed her fist on the roof of his cab when she felt the next round of hysterical tears starting. "Yes, you *are!* You *are* going to help me!" Both hands fumbled at the handle and wrenched the door open before he could anticipate her move. "You're going to *help* me. You *are*. You *are* . . ."

3

A CARPENTER WAS hammering. No, not a carpenter. His apprentice. Drive and miss. Drive and miss.

Craig dug his elbow into the chair arm just so. With the side of his head supported by the heel of his hand, the hammering pain lessened. When he first woke up, the pressure inside his skull had made him almost violently ill. He could get out of bed in a day or two, the nurse had told him. Until then, he was to stay quiet.

He'd waited until the woman had finished her long list of orders and left to deliver more general-like commands to the rest of her patients. She really didn't have any idea what she was talking about, anyway.

He'd made it to Sonia's room. Walking up a flight of stairs and down a corridor hadn't been the easiest project he'd ever taken on, but it was hardly impossible.

Sonia's black curls were nestled on the pillow; stark white sheets were tucked under her chin. Her bed was right next to the chair he had collapsed into. Pale morning light was gradually infiltrating the hospital room; in another hour the rays would reach her curled-up form on the bed.

She *was* curled up, her knees nearly touching her chin, cocooned under the sheet in the fetal position. The position where one was safe...

Craig tried to shift and couldn't. Whoever had kicked his kidneys should enter a competition for skill at the craft. The two cracked ribs weren't bad. They only hurt when he breathed. The broken nose he found almost

24

humorous. When he'd looked in a mirror, he'd found that his whole face had been rearranged. The flesh around one eye was vaguely purple; a spot on the opposite cheek was green and swollen.

None of that was of any serious concern to him. His post-concussion head was another matter. He couldn't think, and he needed to think, but that carpenter's apprentice kept hammering. If he moved too fast, he was annoyingly aware he would be sick.

Sonia shifted just slightly, her eyes fluttering open and then closing again. Her face was lovely in sleep, flushed and soft and vulnerable.

Vulnerable . . . the word twisted like a new pain, this one not in his head. Guilt and rage lanced his heart. The same picture kept materializing in his mind. A tall, lanky blond punk with strange light eyes, wearing dark, filthy jeans and a dark shirt. Young. Thick jowls and not much of a chin, a thin, arched nose.

He'd been working on a mental picture of the bastard for the last two hours, until it was exactingly clear, until he was positive of every detail. Yes, it had been dark, but the moon had been full and the park had had lights. Craig was sure he would know the filthy bastard again. Pianist's fingers, long and thin. For the rest of his life, he would remember the shape of that hand on Sonia's stomach, her horrified cringe at the cur's touch, the sick helplessness in her eyes.

Craig closed his own eyes. *He* was the one who had let it all happen. Skipped out on the bodyguard. Taken Sonia where he knew there was potential danger. A city park, dammit. Charming in the daytime but—he should have known—risky at night. But he'd had it with the asphalt jungle, and had been hungry for grass and trees and privacy. The lake had beckoned . . .

No excuse. He had no excuses for himself.

His mother had died when he was nine; his father when he was seventeen. Craig had fended for himself and fought tooth and nail to make the ranch solvent.

Shale, rich in oil, lay under his grazing land, and at the time he found it, the government had been willing to back anyone who could develop a process for extracting oil from shale. Craig knew as much about oil extraction as every other rancher in the area: nothing. Hard and fast, he learned. Hard and fast, he'd learned everything. For years, he'd needed no one, though the tough, hard veneer had worn off once he was old enough, and experienced enough, to no longer need a protective wall around himself. He'd never been able to define precisely his attitude toward Sonia. He'd played a long, wide field before he met her. With no other woman had he ever felt such intense, instinctive surges of protectiveness.

Sonia was vulnerable. He loved that in her. She believed in people, in their basic goodness; she had such perception and compassion and love in her. The first time he'd touched her, he'd felt a violent urge to destroy anyone who would hurt her, who would dare to harm her. She delighted in teasing him that she'd "been around." She'd been around like a newborn kitten without claws. Her trust—that gut trust that came from the sweetest core of her—she'd never given to anyone before him.

He'd failed to earn that trust last night.

"Craig."

His eyes blinked open. Her sleepy ones met his, soft and shadowed, wrenching his heart.

"Good morning," he whispered. He had to use both hands to get up from the chair, and ignored the apprentice going wild in his head at even slow-motion efforts. He leaned over to kiss her cheek. "How's the shoulder?"

"Fine. Maybe a little sore. Everything's . . . fine, except that I feel pumped full of drugs." She smiled groggily, and then frowned. "Honey, what on earth are you doing here? You're supposed to be flat on your—"

He motioned to the empty bed next to her, his choice of where he preferred being flat on his back totally clear.

Sonia's smile was sleepy. "This is the *women's* ward."

"I like women."

"You'd better not. You're already in trouble with me, Mr. Hamilton."

"Oh?" He made it back to the chair when he felt he could no longer stand, tugging it closer to her bed so he could touch her.

"You all but promised to make love to me last night," she joked groggily. "Lord, what a tease. What kind of way was that to end the evening?"

"A frustrated one," he said wryly.

Slowly, she eased herself up to a sitting position, letting the sheet fall to her waist. The hospital gown made her figure disappear; she looked ten years old with her disheveled mass of blue-black curls and huge turquoise eyes.

Totally disoriented from the sedatives the doctor had pumped into her, Sonia was finding it a monumental task to concentrate. "Craig, you have a concussion—"

"A light one," he lied.

"Did they tape the rib?"

He shook his head. Slowly. "They don't always do that anymore. It's nothing, Sonia."

It wasn't *nothing*. As her vision cleared, she could see the terrible bruises, and beneath his natural tan there was a grayish pallor that terrified her. She reached over to touch his fingers. Their hands matched, forming a tent, fingertip to fingertip. "If you don't lie down, I'm going to tickle you till you cry uncle," she whispered.

Slowly, he raised himself up to a standing position. "You need breakfast. And coffee."

He reached behind her to push a button near the head of her bed. She saw the tiny row of perspiration beads break out on his forehead at that small effort, and wanted desperately to force him to lie down. But how? His eyes had a strange, haunted cast to them she'd never seen before, something that was more than the physical pain she knew he must be suffering. She felt as helpless to do anything for him as she had the night before.

Of their own volition, her fingers groped at her neck.

"Where's my . . . they took my opal!"

His jaw turned to stone. "I know, honey. The nurse will be here in a moment."

"I'm perfectly fine." But she wasn't. Memories of last night flooded through her with sudden dizzying speed, and the sedative hangover only accented those nightmare images. "How could they? How could they take my opal?" Such a stupid thing to say, such a stupid thing even to think. It was just . . . she had always been a giver. No one had ever taken anything from her—no one had had to; there had never been anything she hadn't been willing to give freely for the asking. The opal seemed a symbol of other things the blond bastard had threatened to take— although he hadn't really touched her. He'd only touched the opal, something personal and precious to her, something that could never be retrieved.

Suddenly, she recalled all too clearly her unforgivable hysteria, the burst of uncontrollable crying that had started once she'd gotten Craig safely into the hospital the night before. Why *then,* when she was finally certain he would be all right? Her own loss of control had felt alien and strange, and for an instant she felt that terrible panic again.

Until Craig's hand linked warmly in hers, until his lips came down on her cheek. The anguish in his eyes . . . was *her* fault. His touch was soothing, sensual, reassuring. So like Craig. She blinked back the tears and pressed his hand with a small smile. "They looked like a rock group. I may permanently take up classical music," she whispered.

"Just don't take up country." His palm brushed her cheek, then lazily pushed back her hair. Her heart gradually stopped pounding.

"I thought you liked country music."

"I thought you liked classical." His fingers stopped their slow caress. One forefinger tapped her nose, then poked at the neckline of her hospital gown. "I hope you didn't pay too much for this," he commented.

She chuckled. "You're forever knocking my taste in clothes."

"You have excellent taste, and you know it." He paused. "It's a little different from the satin thing you *tried* to put on a few nights ago."

"Whose fault was it that I never got it on?" She smiled again. "Listen, buster. I got in late last night. This was the only room in town. Degenerate place. They don't even stock toothbrushes."

He leaned over her, his dark eyes glinting with something beyond that haunted pain. Those eyes came toward hers slowly, until firm, soft lips touched hers. "We'll get you your toothbrush," he murmured, "but in the meantime you smell sweet and you taste sweet, love, even in the morning. Must be the reason I married you."

"I thought it was my legs." She raised her hand, ever-so-gently touching the multicolored bruises on his face. He had a Band-aid on his nose, but that was all. Come to think of it, how on earth would they put a nose in a cast? She was not going to cry. Deliberately, she smiled, and she intended to keep on smiling until it snowed in the tropics, unaware that there was a rainbow cast of brilliant moisture in her eyes.

"Silly, it was your eyes. What on earth makes you think I married you for your legs?"

"Listen, Hamilton. I have to take credit for my legs. God knows I wasn't built like Mae West upstairs."

"What fun would it be being married to a life jacket?"

"Lord, I've trained you well," Sonia marveled.

"Very well. And in the meantime, I certainly hope you didn't marry me for my nose."

She chuckled again. "I did." She cocked her head, studying him. "But I guess you'll still do. It'd be too darn much trouble breaking in someone new."

He heaved a weary sigh. "So you want to watch me tie you down and take a feather to your feet?"

When the nurse walked in, Sonia was grateful. The banter had set at a distance the horrors of the night before, but other realities were intruding with frightening speed. Craig was in pain. Serious pain. His movements were achingly slow and his color increasingly ashen. He was giving an Oscar-winning performance, trying to hide the fact that he was hurting, and she loved him with a raving, consuming frustration inside her. *Give in, Craig. Taking on five men. You damn fool. If something had really happened to you, do you think I would have wanted to go on living?*

"*Mister* Hamilton, I really don't believe this." The RN's name was Trether. A tiny white cap was perched meticulously on butter-yellow hair, and the nurse's whites were spotless on a tall, spare figure. "You will be returned to your own bed the very instant I can get an aide in here," she scolded firmly, setting a tray down next to Sonia's bedside. "The doctor will be in your room to see you shortly, and in the meantime Mrs. Hamilton is going to have her shower and eat her breakfast."

Craig didn't even turn around. "You feel up to a shower?" he asked quietly.

"Lord, yes." Sonia was already slipping out of bed. The floor felt cold beneath her bare feet, and so did the provocative draft that sneaked in through the back opening of the hospital gown. Just standing up caused her whole body to ache like the devil, but she knew there was nothing seriously wrong with her. Well, her shoulder was injured. But her concern was all for Craig. She bent over him. "Do what the nurse says," Sonia whispered. "You'll be fed gruel if you don't."

And as she disappeared into the bathroom, Sonia crossed her fingers that he would have no reason *not* to lie down.

It didn't work. When Sonia was behind the closed bathroom door, Craig turned with aching slowness to the nurse. His voice was low, and lethally quiet. "You left my wife *alone* last night."

The accusation, so deadly flat, held more sentencing than a judgment in a court of law. Nurse Trether was taken aback. "Mrs. Hamilton had only to punch the button for any of the nurses to come in here if she'd needed the least thing."

"I *told* you under no circumstances to leave her alone."

The gently teasing, softly reassuring man who'd deliberately chased away Sonia's memories was gone. Back was the commanding, determined man who'd risen from orphan to self-made engineer of a kind. A man who never backed down, not for a principle, never from a fight.

The nurse sucked in her breath at his tight, cold stare. "Mr. Hamilton, I intend to call the doctor immediately. You were told unequivocally to stay in bed. You shouldn't even have been able to make it up here."

"They X-rayed her shoulder last night."

"We told you. It's dislocated. She'll be uncomfortable for a while, but then she'll be perfectly fine." The nurse, about to say something else, rapidly changed her mind.

In four long strides, she reached Craig before he fell.

He woke up four hours later in the men's ward, to find a familiar, wizened little man peering at him worriedly from the far corner of the hospital room.

"Charlie," Craig managed to croak.

The man immediately surged forward. "About time you quit napping. Though I admit the plane trip in the middle of the night was worth it just to see your face. You haven't been in a brawl since I can remember."

Craig half smiled for his old friend. Charlie Adams had more wrinkles than a raisin, habitually looked cranky, and had been thirty-nine for more than a dozen years. Still, anyone who judged Charlie only by his tiny stature was a fool. Behind those puppy-brown eyes was a loyalty that could move mountains and victory over the alcoholism that had nearly destroyed his life—until Craig came along. For the last eight years or so, Charlie had managed Craig's ranch and his house, and since the marriage, occasionally Sonia.

"I suppose I should ask you how you're feeling,"

Charlie remarked, clearly bored with the thought.

"Don't bother." Craig shifted up against the pillows, wincing in a way he never would have in front of Sonia. "You should have woken me when you came in."

"Like hell." Charlie drew a cigar from his pocket, looked at it, and disgustedly put it back in his pocket after reading the no smoking sign over the door. He stuck his hands in his pockets, staring worriedly at Craig. "You need some things? I mean, don't tell me you dragged me all this way to talk business. You know I've got everything taken care of, and you'll be in here at least a few more days."

"I'll be out of here by tomorrow," Craig corrected, and took a painful breath, leaning back against the head of the metal bed. "I need some help here, though, first."

They'd taken the phone out of his room. He wanted to know if the incident was going to be in the press, and if it was, he wanted the papers kept from Sonia. He didn't want her reminded of what had happened, and he wanted to ensure that no one bombarded her with questions about it, either.

The police were supposed to be in later that day. Craig was already afraid of how that was going to go. In a city of three million people, tracking down five rather nondescript hoodlums wasn't going to be duck soup. Not to mention that Chicago's Finest probably had bigger priorities than hunting for petty muggers.

"So?"

"So . . . I want the bastard caught," Craig said flatly. "The whole gang, forget it. But I want the leader found. Hire someone, Charlie; get him out to the park today, and then bring him back to me. I can give him an exact description."

Charlie shook his head, not liking the idea at all. "That's crazy. At least give the police a chance."

"Every chance," Craig agreed. "But do it, Charlie." An almost mischievous smile creased his lips. "I'm sick. You have to cater to me."

"You should be so sick." But Charlie nodded reluctantly.

Craig had other requests. He wanted Charlie to check them out of the hotel, gather their clothes, arrange for plane reservations and transportation to the airport.

"You have something against following the doctor's orders?" Charlie wondered idly. "What exactly is so wrong with room and board here for the week?"

"I want Sonia home." Away from every memory of the night before, away before the story could break in the newspapers. In the country, at home, he could ensure that she would forget the horror of their *Walpurgisnacht*. And back in Cold Creek, he would try to make up to her for what he had *let* happen . . .

The color had drained from his face; his friend apparently noticed. Charlie's hands left his pockets, and he buttoned his old cord jacket. "I got orders only to stay in here for no more than fifteen minutes. I've already been here more than an hour. I'll come back for visiting hours tonight."

"Don't go yet," Craig said wanly, and hated that weak sound in his voice. Dammit, how long was the headache going to last? "There's a man. Peter Farling."

"Never heard of him."

Charlie worried about Craig dealing with people Charlie didn't know.

"He's a jewelry designer. I need a necklace."

"Today?" Charlie said blandly. "Sure you do. Now be a good boy and lock the door so no one else sees you looking like a punching bag."

"Charlie."

He would do it. Craig relaxed when his friend left, and closed his eyes again. Peter Farling had designed the original opal and onyx necklace. And Charlie was the kind of man who didn't ask why Craig needed a necklace in a hurry.

For a long time, Craig lay with his eyes closed. Sleep wouldn't come. The new necklace would make up for nothing. Oh, in his rational mind, he knew Sonia would be all right. She was resilient and optimistic by nature, and he knew that, given time, she really would forget the details of the incident. Once he had her home with him, around places and things they both loved, away from pressures, he would see to it that the open wound scarred over quickly.

Whether *he* could forget it—and forgive himself— was another thing. The irrational part of him was well on the way to becoming obsessed with a memory.

4

SONIA SET DOWN the watering can and wiped her damp, grimy hands on the seat of her cutoffs. Tight velvet buds were just starting to form on the rose stems. Her favorite was the rich apricot-colored one, the one she had grafted herself and the one she had never really believed would work.

Absently, she brushed the trail of moisture from her forehead with her sleeve. Her shoulder just slightly protested the movement with a twinge of stiffness, but not much. Two weeks had made a difference.

Just being home had made the real difference.

Even with the slanted windows open, it was unbelievably hot in the narrow greenhouse. As much as she loved her roses, they refused to thrive under Wyoming's baking sun and endless, driving winds. Charlie and Craig had put the building up two years before, over her repeated protests that she and Craig were away too much for her to spend the time with her favorite hobby. The two men had ignored her—their favorite pastime—and now they were both clearly to blame for the dirt under her fingernails, the hair curling wildly around her cheeks, and the luxurious relaxation she felt after digging in the rich black dirt for the last two hours. Bending down, she scooped up the puppy that had cheerfully untied her shoe strings twice.

The tawny golden retriever pup stared at her with limpid eyes. "You're a disgrace," Sonia informed him affectionately. "All wrinkles. Clumsy. Your paws are

just about bigger than your whole body. And I'm supposed to sell you as the pick of the litter?"

The pup's soft pink tongue lapped lovingly at her
neck. "And I'm never going to be able to give you up.
Craig *did* remark that I was the last person alive who
should try to raise dogs." She set the pup down, tying
her canvas shoes for the third time. With help.

From the open windows, Sonia could just barely hear
the sound of voices from the yard. Smiling, she put away
the trowel and small spade, then rinsed her hands. A
burst of feminine laughter outside made her chuckle.

Some husbands disliked their mothers-in-law. Perhaps
because Craig had lost his mother so young, he had taken
on Sonia's mother like a second chance. The Rawlingses
had lived in Cold Creek for generations, and though
Sonia and Craig had spent the last few years more or
less hopping around with his work, Cold Creek was where
they'd built their home. Both valued those roots, and her
parents had become his adopted ones.

With the pup in her arms, Sonia checked the temperature in the greenhouse and pushed open the door.
Forest smells assaulted her nostrils. Craig's land was
nestled at the fingertips of the massive Tetons. The really
high peaks were miles away, but most of Craig's ranch
sprawled out in a valley nestled among the foothills,
verdant and green and rolling. "Their" river was also a
gift from the mountains, clear and always cold, winding
lazily in and around the property like a silver ribbon.

South of them was a much more arid rolling prairie,
where most of the ranchers around Cold Creek made their
living. And many miles farther southeast was the Green
River Basin, where some fifteen years ago the government had gotten all excited about shale oil. Craig's ranch
worked horses, not oil, but the south end held some of
that shale. Enough for one brash young man with a faint
mustache to experiment with, as pretty much everyone
else in the area had rushed to experiment. The kid in
oversized cowboy boots had had the sense to patent his

oil extraction process, and the rest of his story was the history of one bankrupt ranch's evolution into a successful enterprise dominated by a man who expected to work hard for everything he had. Those boots more than fit him these days.

The ranch was still home to both of them, no matter how far they traveled. Sonia knew exactly what the land meant to Craig. Roots, privacy, quiet, the memory of just how hard he'd fought to save it . . . She drew strength from their home as he did, was renewed by it as he was.

Except—not this time. The phone hadn't stopped ringing since they'd arrived. The rest Craig needed so badly hadn't been given to him. After the weeks of trying to browbeat him into taking it easy and still feeling foolishly jumpy herself whenever she heard a strange sound, Sonia had capitulated that afternoon and called in the troops.

June Rawlings was a very capable one-woman army, a trim attractive woman in white slacks and top, with her daughter's dark hair and long legs. She grinned as Sonia approached. "Good Lord. Look what the pup dragged home this time," she drawled to Craig.

"Thanks," Sonia told her mother wryly, and made her way to Craig's side. She was delighted to see her overworked husband stretched out on a chaise longue. Just an hour and a half of sitting still had put the mischief back in his dark eyes. Not that she particularly appreciated their focus at the moment. His eyes skimmed deliberately over the smudged dirt on her knees, noted the way her halter top stuck provocatively to her slim curves, and sparkled at the errant curls full of their own ideas about hairstyle. "And you can just stop looking at me that way. I'll take a shower just as soon as I've had a drink," she scolded him.

Settling the puppy on his lap, she leaned over for a kiss. Under her mother's watchful eye, a mere peck was protocol, but there was enough time for a solicitous inventory. The bruises and swelling were gone from his face; the bump on his nose wasn't, but she was growing very fond of that odd bump. Bumps didn't matter; it was that tense broodiness she caught too often on his face that worried her. She relaxed. Even her most critical eye could see he was for once relaxed. In fact, Craig was looking a ton healthier each day. He also tasted delicious.

Sonia was suddenly hungry.

"I hope you didn't take that outfit with you when you went to Chicago," her mother said wryly.

Between the two chaise longues was a small metal table with a pitcher of iced tea. Sonia poured herself a glass. "You *could* ask me how the roses are going," she suggested to her mother. In several long gulps, she finished half the tea, and lazily collapsed in the grass between the two lawn chairs. Immediately, the pup bounded down from Craig's lap to pounce on her, causing the glass to tilt and iced tea to dribble on Sonia's knee, in no way contributing to her dignity.

"That's her father's daughter, you know," June told Craig. "I can't tell you how often we thank God you took her off our hands. I never could figure out what you saw in her."

"The legs, Mom."

June shook her head at him. "Those knees are her father's, too. Not mine." She catalogued the parts of Sonia's body, dividing them up genetically and blaming all physical and character deficiencies on her father's genes. What her mother failed to point out, Craig inevitably discovered. Used to such teasing, Sonia ignored both of them. And weary of retying her tennis shoes, she simply pulled them off and arched her hot feet in the soft, cool mat of grass. The puppy promptly lost interest in shoestrings and decided to teethe on her toes.

Before long, a half-dozen more wrinkled, scampering puppies attacked her. Their dam, Tawny Lady, having led out her brood, trotted briskly to Craig's side. His arm went around her, stroking her fur, while Sonia was assaulted unmercifully by their champion retriever's off-spring.

"Come over here and do your own baby-sitting," she ordered Tawny Lady, laughing.

The bitch turned her head and closed her eyes, clearly uninterested in leaving Craig's side. Though she was basically obedient and gentle, there was still no question she was Craig's dog.

"You could always keep them penned," her mother suggested dryly. "Particularly since they're going to be sold eventually; they're not just pets."

"They like to be free," Sonia protested.

June exchanged a look with Craig. "You're to blame for this, you know. You encouraged her to breed this litter. I couldn't believe it at the time."

The pup did a somersault trying to get into Sonia's lap, upsetting the last of the iced tea over her. Shaking her head in despair, she stood up and set the empty glass on the table. "I'm being *driven* to take a shower," she complained.

Her mother chuckled, standing up as well. "I'll go with you as far as the greenhouse to see how your roses are coming, but then I have to go home. Your father will be wondering where I am. No—" She motioned Craig back down. "Don't get up. We've worked too hard being lazy this afternoon to spoil it now."

Craig half closed his eyes. "Tell your daughter to put on something sexy after her shower."

"I'll do that," June agreed.

Mother and daughter exchanged glances on the sloped walk back to the greenhouse. Sonia opened the door, and the two of them disappeared inside. "So that's how you do it, is it?" she asked her mother wryly. "By accusing him of being lazy? If I'd suggested he sit still for a minute, he would have tried to jog forty miles."

"Men." Her mother grinned. The two of them shared a chuckle of mutual understanding. Though they'd seemed at loggerheads when Sonia was growing up, a special closeness had developed as she matured and learned to relate to her mother woman-to-woman.

"The farm going okay?" she asked.

"Mmm. Fine. Need a rain, but then we always need a rain in June." Sonia had inherited her love of roses from her mother, who now studied her daughter's plants with a critical eye, poking a hand into the soil to rub the texture between two fingers. Both knew, though, that the visit to the greenhouse was only an excuse to steal a few minutes together. "He's fine, Sonia," June said absently. "Or he will be. I can see his ribs still hurt him when he moves, but that's to be expected."

"He still gets these terrible headaches," Sonia worried.

"But that was no small concussion. Two weeks isn't so very long."

"If I could get him to stay off his feet more..."

They closed the door on the greenhouse, and Sonia walked her mother to the car. "He's just like your father," June commiserated. "Men are sheer nuisances when they're ill." She paused. "Every blasted last one of them, I believe." She gave her daughter an affectionate, if gingerly, peck on her smudged cheek. "Your roses are doing beautifully. Coffee grounds, Sonia, just a few grains sprinkled around them a few times a week. The plants like that acid. And *stop* worrying. You two are such a pair! He's worse than you are, grilling me four times over the minute you're out of sight about whether you're *really* feeling all right. Now it's time both of you put the incident behind you."

"Hmm."

"Smile," her mother ordered.

Sonia smiled. "Go away. I hate good advice." Laughing, June got into the car. Sonia leaned through the window to hug her mother. "Give Dad a kiss for me, would you?"

Charlie, with a fork poised over a sizzling frying pan, shot Sonia a sardonic look. "It's going to rain, you know."

"It is not." The tray was already on the kitchen counter.

She drew out two Cornish hens from the refrigerator and put them on the tray, then added silverware, salt and pepper, a chilled bottle of wine, and two glasses. "Now what else do we need?" she asked absently.

"A night with no wind. That is, if you plan to cook those outdoors over a fire. If you plan to eat them raw, won't make no difference."

"The wind is going to die down, the minute we go outside," Sonia informed him.

"Oh. That's different, then." Charlie nodded sagely. "You're just angling for an invitation."

"Are you joking? I got a pan-fried steak and *Magnum, P.I.,* coming on. Besides, the minute I saw the wine on the tray I had you figured for being 'in the mood.' Sure do hope Craig had a nap this afternoon."

Sonia picked up the tray. In spite of herself, she felt color rising in her cheeks. She opened her mouth to make a fitting retort, then closed it. Charlie burst out laughing.

She went outside and closed the sliding glass doors on him, balancing the tray precariously on one arm. Charlie was . . . irrepressible. If she didn't love him so much, she'd be inclined to muzzle him.

He didn't, at least, live in the house; he just cooked there. Not that Charlie's bunkhouse didn't have a fully equipped kitchen, but he and Craig had been talking "ranch" over meals for so long that Charlie was more than half family, and besides, she had learned a great many secrets about her husband while chopping onions with Charlie.

Occasionally, he had the misguided notion that he could outthink her, which was totally untrue. Sonia set the tray on the patio table and anchored the napkins with the silverware against the puffing breeze.

Warm fingers of air ruffled her dark curls and teased at the open throat of her white satin blouse. The full sleeves billowed above the tight cuffs, and she could feel that most impertinent wind sneaking beneath the smooth material to her bare skin.

Craig loved her "pirate blouse." When they were alone.

It was one of several garments in her closet that he preferred she not wear in public. At the moment, it was cinched at her waist with a scarlet scarf, above her favorite jeans and her bare feet. The wind was whipping away her perfume, she thought irritably, as she picked up the tray again.

Charlie could think what he liked. She'd only worn the blouse because it was a favorite. Lots of times she felt like dressing as if she were a wanton Gypsy.

Craig could see his wanton Gypsy approaching as he spread the blanket out on the riverbank. The sunset was behind her. The mountains were behind her. Their house, a wandering design of glass and stone, was behind her. Sonia was part of all of it. The soft flame and fire in the sunset was very like her: she had that fresh, untamed core, that soaring ever upward quality that was intrinsically part of the mountains; and she'd fussed over every stone in the house, just as he had, when they'd built it together.

She could have looked more beautiful; he just didn't see how. Curls were bouncing wildly around her cheeks; she was flushed and smiling, and there was a devil-spark of laughter in her eyes as she set the tray down on the ground near him. "I suppose you don't believe we're going to be able to cook anything in this wind."

"Did I say that?" He'd managed to start the fire through sheer willpower. By some miracle, it was holding on to life, its flames licking high in the air, sparks flying toward the river.

"You're a doubting Thomas. Just like Charlie. I'll collect more kindling, and by the time I get back, the wind will have completely died, you'll see. You just stay right there—no," she corrected herself. "You open the wine. I'll be back in a jiffy."

She raced off before he could say anything, and a slash of a smile touched his lips. Naturally, she'd darted away; she was afraid he was going to call off their cookout simply because a dozen dark, clotted clouds were rolling in low and the wind was bringing in a storm with dizzying speed. She'd misjudged him. He wasn't about to rain on her parade; the skies were going to do that all on their own.

He had his eyes full, in the meantime. With hands loosely on his hips, he just watched her. Her breasts were clearly outlined as she walked into the wind; her steps were lithe and free. She had a way of tossing back her head as if she were vibrating with the sheer joy of being alive.

Woods bordered on the riverbank, a tall, heavy stand of pine and hardwoods. The wind tossed up the branches and crooned a whispering song through the leaves. He saw Sonia look up suddenly, and his smile died.

She loved the woods; she always had, and they were safer here than anywhere on earth. A fleeting, haunted fear still touched her features, and then the ghost of a shiver ran through her before she squared her shoulders and entered the shadowy stand of trees. That slight terror wouldn't have passed over her before the incident in Chicago. She'd never associated isolation with vulnerability.

She hadn't known fear before. Rarely did it show on her face, but he'd caught passing glimpses of it in the last two weeks. She'd wake up trembling in the middle of the night, or she'd be reading and all of a sudden touch her throat. . . . They were only isolated incidents, moments. Rationally, he knew they were to be expected. She never mentioned them. But every time he saw that shadow of terror on her face he felt guilt tear at his stomach and rip straight through him.

Sonia emerged from the darkening forest, her arms loaded with twigs. She dropped them all in a haphazard pile next to him, adding a sigh and a chuckle for her efforts. "You only have to do one thing. Pick out two of those that we can use as spits. The last time I chose our makeshift spit, if you'll recall—"

"The chickens ended up in the fire."

A quick crackle of lightning slashed overhead. "Stop that," Sonia ordered the sky mildly. She added several sticks to Craig's fire, then turned to pick up the wine bottle, flicking back her hair. "What on earth have you been doing? You didn't even open this, lazy one." She glanced up with a teasing smile, to find Craig's eyes, piercing dark, on hers. "What's wrong?"

"Nothing. You cold?"

"Nope. You?" She searched his face one more time, but the dark look was gone. His half-smile was easy, very much Craig, and his eyes had possessively fixed on the second button of her blouse. The one she hadn't fastened. No man with eyes that busy could conceivably be brooding. You will instantly stop worrying, she scolded herself. As her mother had said that afternoon, they both needed just to *forget* those hours in Chicago.

Twisting the corkscrew, she opened the wine with a pop. A moment later, she handed Craig his glass, licking her fingers as she grinned at him. "I love Chablis."

"You love cherry soda pop, too," he teased.

"I *crave* cherry pop," Sonia said feelingly. "Probably because Mom refused to buy it when I was a kid. It's so nice to be married. One can indulge in all the forbidden vices . . ."

"Like cherry pop."

"That heads the list, but there are a few others. You probably think I married you for all the mature reasons, like being in love with you, wanting to have your kids, knowing I had to spend the rest of my life with you." Sonia flopped down next to him, her hand expressively dismissing those issues as trivia. "Marrying you was strictly an indulgence, an excuse to give in to all my vices."

"Are you calling me a vice?" Craig demanded.

"Definitely." She regarded her vice with a critical eye. He was wearing old jeans and a shirt she'd twice tried to sneak from his closet to throw in the rag bag. He probably loved the old frayed thing because he knew it made him look like a sex object. The worn blue cotton was soft, stretching across his chest, showing off solid sinew and all that lean toughness that was part of Craig.

"I see when it really counts, talk's cheap. I'll cook dinner, you said, and instead you're just standing there looking sexy and I'm bending my poor cracked ribs."

She flushed and hurried forward, delighted he was joking about the injury. "Would you like another one or two?"

"Cracked ribs? If you're in a wrestling mood, woman, I'm certainly not going to disappoint you." He gave her a threatening look, all dark, thunderous brows. "I'll go in for finger wrestling right after dinner. *If* I get a handicap."

Chuckling, Sonia ordered him down to the blanket and started cooking dinner. It was pitch dark before the fire was really crackling, shooting up tiny orange sparks to the sky as the Cornish hens crackled and browned on the makeshift spit. The wind, as Sonia had promised, died completely by the time they were both pulling off bits of succulent meat with their fingers, devouring their dinner with relish. The knives and forks she'd brought were forgotten; it was too much fun playing Tom Jones.

They rinsed their hands in the river afterward, and both sank back on the blanket, too replete to move. Total silence surrounded their mountain valley. The river picked up the reflection from the dying fire—picked it up and magnified it in a series of repeated images on its black surface.

"Why did we buy that gas grill?" Craig wondered aloud.

"I haven't any idea. We never use it." Sonia curled on her side with her head resting in the palm of her hand. Craig was stretched out, a second blanket bunched up beneath his head. "Everything tastes better by a fire down here," she said contentedly.

He stretched out an arm and motioned. With a chuckle, she edged closer, careful of his battered ribs, finding a home for her cheek in the crook of his shoulder. "Are you hurting?" she whispered.

"No."

She gave him a wry look, tilting her face up at him, her features golden by firelight. "Now, don't get touchy. I haven't asked you once all day."

"You've tried forty-nine times. Sonia..." His thumb gently traced the line of her cheekbone, his eyes suddenly grave. "You've lost a pound or two, haven't you? You're still thinking about what happened."

Her answer came swift and light, determined that he would stop obsessing on the subject of muggers and nightmarish encounters. And if she'd lost a pound or two worrying over him, he'd be the last person alive to know it. "I have been *trying* to lose a pound or two, Mr. Hamilton."

"Why?"

"Why?" She shook her head, her fingers sliding loosely around his waist. "Obviously, because I was getting a little...chunky."

"Chunky?" A rumble of laughter erupted from his chest, echoing in her ear. "You haven't got a chunky bone in your entire body."

"I have, too."

"Where?" He rose up just a little, to investigate her claim. Her thighs certainly didn't have an ounce of fat on them. Her upper arms and shoulders were slim, small-boned. Her tummy was certainly softer than butter beneath the white satin blouse, but there wasn't an extra roll to be pinched. "I can't find any chunks," he murmured, "but I did find something else." He nuzzled the top of her curly head with his chin. "You're not wearing a bra, Mrs. Hamilton."

"I must be."

"I'm quite sure."

"I'm just as sure I put one on."

"I'm quite positive you didn't."

"Must have completely slipped my mind," she said lazily, and closed her eyes. He undid a button, then another, his knuckles softly grazing her smooth flesh. Cymbal crashes and drum-rolls promptly vibrated through her bloodstream.

Two weeks without that ultimate physical intimacy, she thought wistfully. Craig had been so badly hurt. She would have slept in the spare room if he'd let her, wanting him to get his rest, lovemaking the last thing on her mind.

Now, just his teasing touch was enough to make her blood pressure zoom. The problem was that she'd been spoiled. It was so nice being spoiled. Craig was still friend, husband, mate . . . but she missed her lover.

And that thumb of his, flicking slowly back and forth over her nipple, delighting in its responsive tightening, told her that Craig missed her as well. His palms cradled the undersides of her breasts. Cradled, then molded, then kneaded, and a whispered sigh escaped her lips as she arched beneath him.

Craig suddenly tensed, aching in need for her. His lips pressed hard in her hair, then shifted to her temples, exerting enough pressure so that she lifted her face to his, all innocence in loving, her features vulnerable and softly flushed.

An image flashed in his head, an image of her face, contorted with horror and fear, sick with terror. Terror because he'd put her in a position where she could be hurt . . . where she could have been more than hurt. Why hadn't he been alert to the dangers lurking about? The only thing in his head had been the selfish desire to make love with her. Like now. Guilt clawed inside him, so deep and painful that he wrenched his arm free.

"What's wrong?" Sonia took one look at his face and jerked up. "Your ribs, Craig? Oh, darling . . ." Selfish, selfish, selfish, she chided herself. He's hurting like hell and you're going around braless like some hormone-happy harpie.

"The ribs are fine. Sonia . . ."

The fire snapped. They both glanced up. The sky had dropped; swirling masses of charcoal clouds hung just above them. A drop of water splashed down, then another. Both Sonia and Craig bolted up, snatching the tray and blanket and glasses. By the time they started to run for the house, the sky had parted and was dousing them with buckets of water.

— 5 —

BY THE TIME they reached the house, they were both soaked, and laughing. "At least give me credit," Sonia complained. "You notice it didn't rain a drop until we were finished with dinner. I suppose you thought that was nature's doing?"

Craig deposited the tray in the kitchen and, after a quick, token cleanup, led her toward the bedroom. "You're dripping, my talkative one. As soon as you get warm and dry, you can tell me all about your powers over the skies."

"Skeptic. All my life I've been surrounded by skeptics." Sonia groped in the dark for the bedside lamp. Peeling off her wet clothes, she tossed the soaking garments into the bathroom helter-skelter, then pulled on a multicolor caftan that trailed the floor. Her shivers promptly stopped, and she picked up a brush from the dresser.

"Under the covers," Craig ordered.

Muttering about overbearing men, she threatened him with the brush, but dived rather meekly for the blankets, hunching the pillows behind her. "I'm hardly going to catch cold from one little rain."

"Who said anything about your catching cold?" Craig stopped unbuttoning his shirt long enough to press a kiss on her forehead. "I'm just keeping you in your place."

"Bed?"

"Bed," he agreed.

"You think I'm going to put up with that kind of talk?"

49

She leaned back, watching Craig remove the rest of his clothes. The skin around his ribs was still bruised and discolored, and she saw white strain lines under his eyes that she hadn't noticed in the darkness outside. Tugging the covers up to her chin, she again felt angry with herself for being so insensitive as to initiate lovemaking when he clearly wasn't well yet.

He wandered into the bathroom, and Sonia picked up a magazine from the bedside table, but didn't open it. Her eyes roved restlessly over their bedroom. The ceilings were tall and beamed; a stone fireplace took up one corner. The white stuccoed walls had a Spanish flavor; the burnt-orange carpet added a warmth and quiet to the room; and the wall hangings were mixed Sioux and Navaho, in wood-browns and muted oranges and creams, with a hint of pale blue. The room pleased her—it had a rich sensual quality that reflected, she thought with a warm rush, exactly what had always gone on within it. Loving. Not just sex, but affection and closeness, and an intimacy too joyous for laughter, too deep for tears.

Sonia relaxed. Occasionally over the last two weeks, she'd been haunted by the specter of the man who had so badly frightened her in Chicago; yet the longer she was home and around Craig, the easier she found it to put the incident in perspective. However horrible it had been, that episode of less than an hour's duration could not permanently mar the life she had with Craig.

He returned from the bathroom stark naked—but then, he always slept stark naked. He slipped between the sheets next to her, readjusted the pillows behind her as if she weren't perfectly comfortable the way she had them, and picked up a magazine from his own bedside table. "Are you warm enough?"

"Sweltering, thank you."

His dark eyes flicked over hers possessively. "If only sass could keep you warm."

She chuckled, but her eyes turned serious as she flipped through the magazine. "We're home for a change. I mean, really home. It seems as if we've been hop-skipping everywhere from Washington to Denver for the last couple years."

"Feel good?"

"I've loved it all, but yes, it feels terrific to just be home." She set down the magazine, giving up all pretense of reading, and snuggled on her side. "I talked to Marina on the phone yesterday."

Marina managed the largest department store in Cold Creek, one that catered to customers with excellent taste in clothes. Marina and Sonia were old friends. Several years before, they'd talked about Sonia working in the store; after all, before she was married, she'd had those years at the Denver boutique. Sonia had never had the time to commit to a job with Marina. She and Craig had had a home to build; she'd wanted to travel with her husband and knew she worked well at his side; the ranch itself took time. . . . She'd never been idle.

But the idea of setting up a fashion-consulting service in Marina's store had intrigued her for a long time. The oil boom had increased the number of jobs in Cold Creek, both for men and for women. Women reentering the work force, Marina had told her, felt fashion-nervous. They didn't want to waste their hard-earned dollars on wardrobe mistakes, but were eager to be appropriately dressed in today's career-woman styles. Sonia would be the perfect adviser, Marina had told her often; she had the flair for clothes, several years of experience, and an inimitable way with people.

Wardrobe consultants were nothing new; they had proved successful in larger cities, and Sonia had discussed the job idea with Craig before.

"She wants me to come down there next week," Sonia started to say.

"No," Craig said swiftly.

She glanced up at him in surprise. He'd always supported the idea. Actually, no matter how often he teased her about her clothes, she knew he was proud of her taste—particularly if she could show it off in a world full of women.

With his face turned away from her, he flicked out the light, tossed his magazine aside and slid down lower in the sheets, reaching for her. "I didn't mean to make that sound so harsh," he said quietly. "I just want to see you take it easy for a while, sweet. Loaf. Play lazy lady." His hand stroked her cheek, and then slid down to rest around her waist. "You'd be good at consulting work for Marina, Sonia, and of course you can do anything you want to do. But give it a month or two, won't you?"

"It's not as if anything has to be decided this week," she agreed, and yawned helplessly, sleepiness stealing over her like a silken web. She didn't really object to the thought of a few weeks of doing absolutely nothing for a change. Still, there was a curious note in her voice. She had been so sure Craig would approve of the project, and instead he'd practically jumped in to quash it.

She smelled warm and feminine and soft, snuggling closer to his warmth. Craig's eyes blinked open in the dark, unseeing, his jaw oddly tight. He forced himself to relax. Sonia was never going to be content just sitting home for long; he knew that. To keep her down hadn't been his wish at all, and never would be. But there were a dozen protective eyes on her at the ranch; the idea of her gone all day, vulnerable, among strangers... "Not that I want you to get bored," he whispered. His lips pressed into her hair. "I'm going to the site in the morning. Think you can wake up early enough to come with me?"

"Certainly. Except that you're not going to the site tomorrow. Craig, it's still too soon, you're not—"

"About eight. You haven't been out there in a long time."

She sighed. She *hadn't* accompanied him to work in a long time, primarily because he was so busy there that he barely had time to breathe. She could hear the implacable note in his voice, though, and thought fleetingly that if she went with him she could at least make sure he didn't become overtired.

"You want to go?" he asked.

"I'd love to go."

"You're not going to be cranky if I wake you up that early?"

"I am *never* cranky in the morning," she informed him.

He chuckled. "Sleep," he urged her. "I love you, little one."

Sonia slid a knee between his, settled her arms loosely around his waist, and tucked her head just under his chin. No human being could possibly sleep that way for an entire night, but she couldn't sleep at all if she didn't start out that way.

Craig did his part in the nightly ritual, arranging the comforter to her chin, then sliding his hand slowly down her back to her bottom, where his palm rested on the curve of her hip. Against her stomach, like a warm surprise, was the feeling of his throbbing and most intimate arousal, nurtured by nothing more than the physical closeness between them.

In time, he fell asleep. Sonia cuddled contentedly, waiting for the darkness to claim her as well. Part of Craig remained distinctly unsleepy, still pulsating against her, making her half smile. And then not. Before the attack, she thought fleetingly, a cracked rib wouldn't have stopped his making love to her. *Nothing* had ever stopped his making love to her, almost from the first moment he'd met her. Until now.

Groggily, Sonia wandered into the bathroom, flipping on the faucets for the shower as she wrapped a turban around her hair. Waiting for the water temperature to warm, she was terribly afraid the nice, sleepy euphoria was going to fade the instant she stepped under the pelting spray.

The ominous premonition proved true as she closed

the sliding glass door and felt the pulsing hot water rush over her flesh. Her eyes even opened—a miracle. Through the cloudy glass, her eyes registered all the pale blue and silver features of "her" bath . . . she could hear Craig's disgraceful baritone coming from the "his."

She was the one who'd thought that "his" and "her" bathrooms were critical when they were designing the house. After all, how long could romance last when one had to brush one's teeth in front of one's mate and have an audience for putting on makeup? Not to mention that she had a longtime habit of hanging out her pantyhose to create an obstacle course.

"Sonia? Are you finally up, sleepyhead?"

In principle, next-door bathrooms were a good idea. Except that Craig had modified the original architectural plans when they'd put the shower in. "No," she murmured grumblingly.

A glass door slid open behind her. Not the shower door that she'd just closed, leading into her bathroom, but the glass door that divided their individual shower stalls. Suddenly, there was *nothing* dividing their individual shower stalls; and one very naked, very wide-awake man with wicked dark eyes aimed a hand shower sprayer in her direction, attacking her unmercifully until she was gasping.

"Feel more wide awake?" Craig said mildly. "It's really much easier if you get it over all at once."

"Did you hear me asking for advice? You know, if we ever have a two-year-old, he's going to feel right at home with you."

"You look beautiful."

"I haven't had my coffee."

"Coffee couldn't possibly make you look more beautiful. Sonia, you are delectable in the buff," Craig said gravely.

Color touched her cheeks, and a small smile curled on her lips. "Why can't you just let me be mean and cranky in the morning? Why do you always have to put me in a good mood?" she complained, switching off the faucets as Craig shut off his. Dripping, Sonia brushed deliberately against him on the way out of his shower door, and reached for one of his towels.

That was the other problem with the "his" and "her" bathrooms. Hers was a waste; it was never used. His toothpaste was better, too, and she'd gotten into the habit of stealing his shaving cream when she shaved her legs. Worse than that, she'd unfortunately become addicted to watching the way he vigorously rubbed his hair dry with a thick towel. And besides, she'd stocked his red and gold bath with huge, luxurious scarlet towels, twice the side of those on her side. With his towel wrapped around her, she squeezed his blue and white toothpaste onto her toothbrush, which inevitably seemed to be in there anyway.

"Think you can actually be ready to go in about half an hour?" Craig asked her.

"No problem," she promised him.

She watched in the mirror as he took the towel off his head and leaned with both elbows on the marble counter, regarding her as she brushed her teeth. "Before we were married, I swore I'd never do this in front of you, you know," she told him.

"You were always modest about the silliest things."

"Turn your head."

He did, deftly removing her thick scarlet towel at the same time. In all her naked dignity, she escaped to the bedroom a few minutes later. Ten minutes after that, she was dressed. A short-sleeved black crepe blouse tucked into a black and white checked skirt; red sandals, red button earrings, and a red silk rose on her lapel finished the outfit. She flicked on mascara, whisked blusher on her cheeks, and smoothed on cherry lipstick—all the makeup she ever wore. She might not be awake, she mused, but her husband was still fooling around with shaving cream.

She wandered promptly toward the smell of coffee.

The kitchen was positively drenched in sunlight. Cheerful yellow beams danced on the old Spanish tiles and on the fireplace in the breakfast nook. She closed her eyes, inhaling the aroma of coffee like an addict deprived of his fix, then took the first sip and wandered out of the dazzling brightness with the cup in her hand. One could only take so much cheerfulness this early.

Now, now, you're in a better mood than you're letting on, she chided herself absently. Darn it, you like being married to that man.

So what else was new?

She paused in the doorway to the living room, still sipping her hot brew. The cathedral ceiling gave the room an airy feeling. She'd furnished it with big overstuffed furniture in cream, not at all a practical color for a ranch—but then, they half lived in the kitchen and Craig's den. Eight feet up, a narrow lanai ran along the inside walls; dozens of hanging plants spilled down from that. They were the absolute devil to water, but no arguing from the team of Craig and Charlie could make her give them up. Rugs and wall hangings in brilliant Indian and Spanish patterns added color that caught the morning sun . . . primarily because they'd put so many windows in the room. *More* cheerfulness, she thought wryly.

From those open windows, she had an inspiring view of the mountains, all smoky in the distance this morning. The rain last night, so rare for June, had drenched all the shrubs and greenery she'd planted a few years before. She needed to cut some roses and bring them in, she thought absently. And knew that it wasn't the morning that was making her grumpy, but worry that Craig was overdoing by going back to work so soon, even if it was only for a few hours.

"Ready?"

She whirled. He could not have looked healthier, her husband in his conservative white shirt with navy and gray patterned tie. A suitcoat hung over his arm, matching his gray pants. He had on his tough go-to-work expression; a no-nonsense attitude radiated from his lithe stride. At least until his eyes appraised her from head to toe.

"Now, black and white is very conservative," she informed him.

"Not on you."

"You don't like it?"

"You'll draw eyes," he said flatly. "In the next life, I'm going to marry a little mouse with a sunken chest who wears only brown."

She chuckled. "Don't kid yourself, sexy. You're not going to be rid of me in the next life, either. Not by a long shot."

"You've obviously had your coffee."

"In the next life, *I'm* the one who's going to wake up nice and cheerful; *you'll* be the meanie."

"You'll still be stuck with me," he said wryly, and swung an arm around her shoulder as they headed for the car.

It was an hour's drive to the construction site. Anticipation increased in Sonia as they neared the project. She hadn't been there in months, not only because Craig had been involved in meetings in Washington, but because a site where shale oil was being extracted was hardly the most natural place for a woman to be, unless she wore a hard hat and geologist's boots.

Craig parked the car, viewing his wife's antsy movements with a chuckle. "I have this terrible feeling you have a secret wish to run a bulldozer. Are you going to be able to contain yourself while I work through a few things in the office?"

"What do you pay a bulldozer operator?" she demanded.

"I refuse to answer that."

"You haven't really told me in a long time how the project's been going." She understood the basics. Craig's *in situ* processing method of extracting oil from shale was ecologically sound as well as profitable. That balance had always been the tricky thing. And Craig's method, if anyone asked Sonia, was the only one that really worked.

"How long are you going to be?" she asked him as they walked toward the two-story office building.

"No more than an hour or two."

"I'll just wander around, then."

"No," Craig said swiftly.

Sonia's eyebrows arched up in surprise. "Craig, I don't want to get in your way. You know I'm perfectly happy just poking around. Everyone knows me..."

He obviously wanted her in sight, she thought with amusement. Mrs. Heath met him at the door of his office, her crinkly gray hair standing on end as it always did. Piles of crises had accumulated in his absence, all of which Mrs. Heath politely indicated he should immediately resolve.

She served Craig a cup of coffee, then he went about the business of resolving. John was one of his geologists; his crisis had something to do with the marketing of nahcolite, a by-product of the extraction process. After that, Senator Brown wanted to discuss a section of the Synthetic Liquid Fuels Act that worried him. After *that*, the director of the Bureau of Mines...

Somewhere in midstream her husband seemed to realize he was holding her hand. He didn't *look* the part of a lovesick teenager, Sonia thought with wicked humor; he *looked* very much the man in control. Tough and rough and hard and smart. She divested herself of his hand long enough to wander to the window.

Outside was a barren wasteland of sagebrush with the sun beating relentlessly down on it. It always amazed her that such a short distance from home, green rolling landscape turned into gutted gullies and arid rolls of parched land. The aboveground shale-oil workers always argued that messing up the landscape here was hardly an ecological crime. At first glance, of course, one saw no beauty. At second glance, however, one might see a herd of mule deer grazing on one of the hills, an eagle swooping down, a plant bursting into flower. Even the pitted gullies had their own kind of lonely beauty.

Two tall, gray, windowless structures gleamed silver in the morning sun, and a fleet of large trucks, bulldozers, and cranes was parked by the office. That was all, though. No one could ever guess that three hundred people were probably working underground at this moment, or what was happening there.

Her feet were itching to take the huge elevators down to see what was going on at the heart of the project. She knew the mechanics . . . more or less. Oil was down there; that was a given. In conventional mining, the shale was brought to the surface, and the oil separated from it by a heating process called retorting. That method, unfortunately, left a legacy of slag, polluted water, and air no one would want to breathe.

When the mining was done underground, very little water was required; no air pollution resulted; and the slag presented only minor disposal problems.

It was so simple; Craig had explained it to her a dozen times. Underground, the men dynamited, leaving masses of broken oil shale. The rubble was later exposed to tremendous heat, which caused the oil to separate from the rock. Then the oil was pumped up and sent to the refineries. So simple, to produce a few hundred thousand barrels of oil a day that the country desperately needed . . .

And not simple at all, Sonia thought absently. Meeting energy needs was never simple. Any sudden increase in fuel supplies was enough to send prices plummeting, enough to destroy national economies as well as oil companies. Craig's project received funds from the federal government and from private investors, all of whom had the same goals: to produce fuel in a way that would not upset economic systems, didn't harm the environment, and earned profits. Craig's process was designed to achieve that goal.

Sonia stirred restlessly at the window. She was shamelessly proud of him. When push came to shove, though, she couldn't care less about the project when her husband's health was at stake. She turned and watched him for a moment with ruthlessly critical eyes.

Craig was on the phone; Mrs. Heath was in the doorway; John, in a short-sleeved shirt with his hard hat cockeyed, was leaning over Craig's desk. Her man had loosened his tie twenty minutes ago, rolled up his shirt cuffs even before that. One arm was lazily folded over his ribs, but there were no pain lines around his eyes, no drawn look between his brows that signaled a headache.

And he was busier than a one-armed juggler. Smiling, Sonia slipped toward the door with a wink for Mrs. Heath. She was perfectly content wandering around on her own and hardly wanted to be in Craig's way.

She'd made it to the end of the corridor before she felt a warm hand slip into hers again. She glanced up to find a very handsome man with a shock of brown hair over his forehead and a very clear pair of blue eyes focused on hers.

"That stuff will wait," Craig told her. "I've got things to show you."

He did, she admitted. Her husband had a great many things to show her, in spite of being constantly interrupted by people who needed—and claimed—his attention. His hand still remained irretrievably locked with hers.

The dusty workers from underground, talking about tolerances and heat and percussion problems, must have thought it strange.

So did Sonia. Craig had never before exactly tied her to his wrist while he went through the mundane details of his work. She didn't mind. She'd always liked the simple intimacy of holding hands.

Whither thou goest, I shall go, she thought whimsically. Mr. Hamilton, you're not feeling just a little violently possessive this morning, are you?

She said nothing aloud. He loved her, and sooner or later he'd notice what he was doing. She hoped sooner. She wanted to make a trip to the ladies' room.

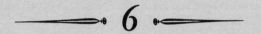

6

"COME ON, CHARLIE. You know you'll have a good time if you come with us," Sonia coaxed. As additional bribery, she handed him a lemon meringue pie to hold, then turned to wrap the bowl of potato salad with plastic wrap. Neither the huge bowl nor the single pie would even dent the hunger of the billions of people she knew her mother had invited for the barbecue; but then, everyone would bring similar offerings. June Rawlings believed in annually celebrating the first of July, for no good reason that anyone worried about.

"I'll just take this out to the car for you," Charlie said gruffly. "But I got too much to do to go anywhere."

She trailed him out to the back of the station wagon, which was already loaded with swimming suits, two root-wrapped rosebushes as presents for her mother, a long skirt to wear later, and some tools Craig was lending her father. She stood back up from the car and blew a wisp of curl from her cheeks. "You're going," she told Charlie with an affectionate and most determined gleam in her eyes. "No more nonsense about being too busy. It's too hot to work; you know my mother will kill you if you don't show up; and you're too darned old to be shy. Furthermore, you're going swimming when you get there."

Charlie gave her a disgusted look and hitched up his jeans. "I'll go swimming when hell freezes over."

"It just did."

"You'll have a fine time without me," Charlie said stubbornly.

"But I won't *have* to have a fine time without you."

Charlie sighed. "You used to be agreeable when you first married him, you know. Now suddenly it's all Miss Bossy and Sure of Herself—"

"Oh, hush."

"Now what are you two arguing about?" Craig demanded from behind her.

"The same thing we've been arguing about all morning." Sonia turned with a sneaky wink for her husband. "If we don't get going, the lemon pie's going to melt. We're not leaving until Charlie gets in the car; the pie's going to be ruined; I'm going to cry—"

"Oh, for godsake," Charlie said disgustedly, and headed for the passenger door. "She could wear down a rock," he mentioned to thin air.

"He probably won't talk to me for the rest of the day— darn it, wait a minute! I'll be right back." Sonia's long legs took her flying back to the house. Her mother had given her an article on rose care that she'd promised to return today.

In Craig's study, she rapidly sifted through the papers on the desk, knowing she'd seen the article there last. Her fingers found the four-page essay, but as she snatched it up, a file folder slid to the floor, spewing papers out.

"Only when I'm in a hurry," she muttered as she bent over. Her hurried movements stilled when her eyes unintentionally caught the few lines of writing on the page. It was a receipt for services rendered—by a man in Chicago.

A faint frown furrowed her brow. The man was an investigator, according to his letterhead. And the money Craig had paid him was not insignificant.

Craig had never mentioned the investigator to her. Actually, in the last few weeks he hadn't said anything at all about the incident in Chicago; she was so sure he had finally put it out of his mind. But this . . .

"Honey?" Craig called from outside.

An odd chill whispered down her spine. Quickly, she shoved the papers back into the file and returned it to the desk, racing with her mother's article back to a pair of impatient men.

"It's perfectly okay that you wanted to take the entire day getting ready," Charlie told her. "I'm holding the melting pie you were so worried about."

"Thank you, Charlie," Sonia said solemnly, and slid into the back seat as Craig started the engine.

"How long are you two going to keep this up?" Craig wondered aloud. His eyes flickered back in the rearview mirror, settling on Sonia's orange camisole with the white satin ribbons that looked terribly precariously tied. Then up, to where her sassy lips curved in a delighted grin.

"It's pinned very securely underneath," she assured him.

"Pardon?"

"Nothing, Charlie."

Sonia leaned back for the ride, stretching out her legs, closing her eyes like a sleepy cat in the sun. Heat seemed to have lethargically replaced blood in her veins. The men maintained a steady conversation in the front seat, but she was only quasi-listening, and her relaxed smile was only partly sincere.

Craig had hired an investigator to find their assailants? She didn't understand. The Chicago police were undoubtedly doing everything they could to find the muggers, and regardless, emotionally and perhaps irrationally Sonia wasn't certain she wanted the culprits found, if it meant she and Craig had to be involved again. The incident was *done,* over with, and nothing could undo it. Dwelling on it accomplished nothing; the image of the blond man with the strange light eyes only raised nausea in her when she did so—nausea and the sick memory of horror, of feeling so vulnerable and fragile . . .

Unconsciously, her fingertips rose to her throat. An opal rested in the hollow there, an opal in an onyx setting with a chain so delicate the gold rested like a whisper on her skin. Craig had replaced the original one more than two weeks ago. She hadn't taken it off since.

She opened her eyes slightly, focusing on Craig in the driver's seat. Love was in her eyes—eyes that were blue-green like the soft shimmer of water at dawn. Love for the man who had clasped that necklace around her throat in the middle of the night without saying a single word. She'd bring up the private investigator's receipt with him sometime, but not now. The last thing she wanted on her mind today was the mugging.

Craig's hair was getting a little shaggy in back, she judged critically. His shirt was white, a short-sleeved knit like a golfer's shirt; her eyes traveled over his shoulders, muscular and taut, sun-bronzed and strong. As he turned to Charlie, Craig was squinting in the bright afternoon sun; she caught his profile, from the smoky gray eyelashes to the slight bump in his nose to the look of his smooth lips. That chin of his jutted out. Not an easy-to-manage chin.

The chin needed kissing. So did the mouth. So did the eyes, the shoulders. All of him, actually. What he needed, Sonia considered gravely, was to be brutally wrestled to the ground, his clothes ripped from him, and very, very soft kisses forced on him, inch by inch.

"Sonia? You remembered the potato salad?"

Her face flushed with color. "It's right here." As they turned into her parents' driveway, she found herself staring at Craig for one more instant. Vitality was beginning to radiate from him again; he exuded energy. And virility. And purpose. His stride was swift and free, no longer inhibited by pain with every movement; the worst of the bruises were gone. His headaches had lasted the longest and still happened sporadically—normal, the doctor had said. But Craig hadn't had a headache in days, not even a twinge. He'd never admitted to having them anyway, but she'd become an expert at knowing the signs.

They still hadn't made love. Sonia had simply dropped

all sexual thoughts from her mind. To encourage that kind of action when he might be hurting again—no. Craig would have to be the judge of when. So it had been a few weeks, she acknowledged. So? Sonia well knew that Craig liked his loving long and lazy. Very long. Very lazy. Very slow, and on occasion terribly, terribly wild...

"Are you sleeping back there?" Craig opened her door, peering in with an amused grin.

Embarrassed, she bolted up and out of the wagon, rapidly snatching up the potato salad as she did. Charlie had already disappeared. Sounds of laughter and conversation rippled toward her from the side of the ranch house, by the pool. The yard was crowded with little people, big ones, old folk and young...and the smell of roasting pig filled the air. Sonia knew her parents must have started the barbecue at daybreak.

The sun filtered down in long yellow waves, dancing on the pool waters, catching the bright colors of the children's bathing suits. Laughter resounded in the air; it was a glorious day for a barbecue.

"I didn't think you were ever going to get here!" June Rawlings descended on them, in white shorts and long legs not unlike her daughter's, her dark hair pulled back with a cheerful red scarf. She swooped down to kiss Craig, then Sonia, then helped them carry their stuff in from the station wagon. "Where's Charlie?" she asked with surprise.

"Mike Henning caught sight of him the moment we drove in. They're already over by the pool," Craig told her.

"That man," Sonia huffed. "Getting him off the ranch takes a bulldozer, and you know darn well we'll have to pry him loose to get him to come home."

"You don't think by any chance think Charlie thrives on all the attention you give him, do you?" Craig asked wryly.

"Nonsense." When Sonia bent over to reach for their

swimming gear, her shorts rode up on her bottom, and then slid down respectably when she straightened.

Craig's eyes darkened. The tightening in his loins was familiar. A certain loneliness ached inside him for the intimate touch of her, yet an unfathomable bleakness etched sudden tension on his features. Thankfully, neither his wife nor his mother-in-law noticed.

"Have we got it all?" June asked. "Sonia, you sweetheart, you didn't have to bring a pie." She gave her daughter an impish grin. "And now we'll have to hide it. If your father catches even a whiff of lemon meringue, you know there won't be a bite left by dinnertime."

"I almost made two." Sonia let out a delighted burst of laughter as two small children came barreling toward her from the long slope of the yard. Rapidly she filled her mother's hands, freeing her own just in time to catch two curly towheads, neither much bigger than knee-high.

"Sonie, go swim! Sonie, go swim!"

"They've been driving Arlene nuts, waiting for you two to get here," June said dryly.

"Do my sister good," Sonia announced. "Where's Uncle Craig?" she asked the youngsters. "Are we going to give him a good dunking in the water?"

Her niece and nephew launched themselves at Craig then, and he carried one child under each of his arms toward the house, both giggling and menacing him with dire threats as soon as they got him in the pool. He threatened them right back, which only made them giggle harder.

They took care of the food, changed into their bathing suits, and greeted the other guests. Arlene fussed for a minute over whether the little ones should be forced to take naps and was hooted down. In the melee of noise and confusion, Sonia found her father. Stephen Rawlings was standing on the front porch with a group of ranchers, holding a glass of lemonade, his weathered face squinting in the sun. He was tall, and his hair was gray these days; a paunch was developing around his middle. And Sonia probably loved him more than life. She collected a kiss and quick squeeze before her husband yelled for her.

"What are we going to do with these urchins now?" he demanded ominously, referring to the one towhead draped over his shoulders and the other hanging upside down in his arms.

For an instant, she wasn't exactly sure what she wanted to do with the children, but knew precisely what she wanted to do to her husband of the bare brown chest and frayed swimming trunks. *Stop that, Sonia.* "First, we're going to throw them in the pool," she announced, and grabbed one warm, wiggling body away from him. The upside-down one. "And *then,* you little troublemakers..."

The July sun beat down in increasingly sultry waves; a horse neighed somewhere in the distance; the smells from the barbecue wafted toward them; the pool waters felt like slinky, cool silk on overheated flesh. It was just that kind of day when all the senses were alive and bursting; Sonia started smiling and didn't stop. First little Johnny swam between her parted legs, then Susie. Sonia's father dropped pennies into the pool bottom for the children to claim. The children bullied Craig into doing a somersault underwater, and then they played keep-away with a beach ball. Sonia, laughing, loved the feel of the warm, wriggling bodies and quickly snatched hugs from her niece and nephew. She adored them. The little devils both knew it.

When at last Arlene showed up at the side of the pool, Sonia was gasping, shaking her head free of water as she handed her niece and nephew over. "Nap," she mouthed to her older sister.

"I actually think they will, now," Arlene whispered back.

"Not *them,* you fool. Me," Sonia complained feelingly.

"Want *Sonie,*" Susie told her mother belligerently, the sound muffled as a towel buried her head. "Want Uncle Craig."

"You only want them because they spoil you to absolute bits," her mother informed her and, with an affectionate grin for Sonia, carried off the two protesting youngsters.

Craig surged up from the water behind her, his arms sliding around her waist as he pulled her back against him. Water suddenly trembled on her skin in the sunlight. She leaned back, eyes closed. Sensuality seemed to be stalking her like a thief in the night. The hardness of his thighs against the backs of hers; the cool, bare skin of his chest rubbing against her spine; the feel of his hands on her flat stomach, barely covered by the simple red maillot. . . . His cheek nuzzled against hers. "I think you want one of those," he mentioned idly.

She glanced up at the children before they disappeared into the house with her sister. "I do," she agreed. They hadn't talked about babies before, not seriously. She had wanted Craig to herself the first years, and then they'd been busy, gallivanting across the country, building their house. . . . She still wanted Craig to herself, but the urge for babies was growing, the need for their own personal exhausting little Hamiltons to worry over and fret about the way Arlene did about her kids.

Sonia turned in Craig's arms, her eyes level with the column of his throat. Water droplets curled in the damp mat of hair on his chest like diamonds in the sun; his skin was cool and wet, his hair slicked back. The urge to touch him, to rub her breasts against him until they ached and tightened. . . . No one would see, she told herself. And knew darn well that everyone would see.

"Sonia?"

He had beautiful eyes. Sexy eyes, as bright as the sky, deep and tender and sweet. His finger curled under her chin, lifting it; she could feel the sudden tautness in his body, a kind of waiting silence as his head bent lower, blocking the sun, coming closer . . .

A neighbor suddenly pitched a ball into the pool, splashing both of them. "Hey, you two! How about a game of volleyball?"

* * *

Dinner was absolute chaos, with adults running helter-skelter, kids dropping their plates on the grass, dogs cavorting in search of scraps. Sunburned faces grinned while butter dripped down chins from the roasted sweet corn.

After dinner, the children did their usual vanishing act, undoubtedly to prevent their parents from whisking them home before they'd finished playing. The grownups changed into grown-up clothes and settled on the chaise longues around the pool with glasses of June's lethal punch. Sonia was stretched out between her mother and sister, holding her second glass of punch, her other hand shielding her eyes against that last brightness of daylight. Craig was standing with a group of ranchers that included her dad.

The sky was filled with puffy clouds, slowly moving across the horizon. Listening absently to her sister's gossip, Sonia kept seeing whimsical pictures in puffs. One looked like the trunk of an elephant; another distinctly like the face of a man. Another, if she observed it just so, looked exactly like a man and a woman in an embrace...

"Where'd you get your skirt, Sonie?"

Sonia glanced at her sister, then down to her white cotton ankle-length skirt with its hem of embroidered orange flowers. The orange matched her camisole, both whimsical purchases for a summer evening a long time ago. "Marina's, I think," she said. "You haven't said how Matt's doing."

"Terrific. I thought at first we'd never get used to living in town, but it's nice. Having neighbors and stores so close...I miss my morning rides, though."

Sonia loved her older sister; she really did. Both her mother and sister filled a very special niche in her life. Craig had become her world with their marriage; her priorities had changed, but there was still occasionally the urge to indulge in simple gossip and chitchat, and her sister was an expert at both. At the moment, though, Sonia couldn't seem to concentrate. She found herself staring at the tiny cubes of ice in her punch glass. Ordinary ice cubes. Two clung together and they looked remarkably like an upturned bottom, naked and smooth.

Good Lord! *Would you stop this?* Restlessly, Sonia stood up, feeling her breasts pushing against the soft camisole material. She was sex-obsessed this evening. "Anyone want some more punch?"

An unfortunate question. Everyone wanted more punch, and they were all too lazy to get up and fetch it themselves. Smiling, Sonia started serving. The problem, she told herself silently and severely, is that out of nowhere you suddenly don't have enough to do. Since they'd been home, Craig had shielded her from his work instead of involving her in it. She didn't mind. Marina had been calling consistently, enticing her with a job she really wanted to do . . . only the next minute all she could think of was how much she wanted a child. It was a perfect time; they were finally settled . . . except in the meantime, she seemed to have little to do but think too much. She wasn't used to inactivity.

She finished serving punch, refilled her own glass, and carried it back with her to the kitchen. Her mother hired help to clean up after the barbecue every year; but the total chaos of the kitchen reached out to Sonia like salvation. Just get busy, she told herself.

In a restless spurt of energy, she tossed out napkins and paper plates and cups, filled the sink with soapy water, washed the empty serving dishes, and started covering what food remained uneaten. People would still come by to pick and nibble, but covering things would at least prevent the food from drying out. See? All better, she told herself as her hands moved with the speed of blades on a fan, picking up, cleaning up, sorting through, covering.

Her lemon meringue pie was gone; she washed the pie pan, then searched for her potato-salad dish. The po-

tato salad, too, had been all but devoured. Just a tiny
smidgen was left, a little hump in the corner that remarkably resembled a certain portion of the male anat-
omy . . .

She dropped the bowl and wearily brushed her fingertips against her temples. Phallic symbols in potato
salad, Sonia. How nice. The men in the white coats are
going to come to put you away.

Craig scanned the cluster of women by the pool, his
eyes resting idly on the empty chaise longue when he
failed to find Sonia. Some inner network inevitably
broadcast an announcement when she wasn't close by.

He'd hadn't been able to keep his eyes off her all day.
A dozen things had captivated him. First, the look of her
long legs swinging around the poolside, then her laughter
as she talked with people, and last the loving softness in
her eyes as she played with the children.

He'd watched her moving through the pool, a graceful
darting fish in the red maillot bathing suit, her hair sleek
against her scalp, her face turned up to the sun. Later,
in that quiet time after dinner, she'd moved ever so softly
in the long skirt that swayed around her legs. She was
always his softer, quieter Sonia when she dressed that
way . . .

He was going to have to get over his habit of falling
in love with his wife over and over again on a daily basis.
In the meantime, he missed her. Excusing himself from
the other ranchers, he wandered toward the house. The
sun had just set, and a glow of scarlet and violet bathed
the ranch yard and pool in a sensual glow.

He knew all about sensual glows. Sonia had been
radiating them all day with that certain look in her eyes—
like Eve, pelting him with apples. Like Adam, he could
only be so strong.

Desire had been tearing through him for more than a
month. He couldn't think of a time in their marriage that
they'd gone more than a few days without making love.

He was the reason for their abstinence; his physical health, Sonia believed. Only that wasn't the reason at all.

Silently, he pulled open the screen door and let it close quietly behind him. No one was in the old ranch house; he wandered through the living room and hall, pausing only when he reached the doorway to the kitchen.

Her skin was slightly damp, glowing and golden from the heat; her camisole was molded to her high, firm breasts. The white skirt swayed around her hips as she fussed around the kitchen, her face still turned away from him. She'd lost her shoes somewhere, and her bare toes peeked out from beneath the skirt hem. She looked sensual and sexual and beautiful and totally touchable, every texture that was Sonia soft and vibrantly warm and all woman.

"Craig!" She flushed still deeper at the sight of him and then quickly turned her eyes away, as if embarrassed, as if afraid he might guess what she'd been thinking.

"Ready to go home?" he asked her. He knew exactly what she'd been thinking. And it was past time to go home and take care of his wife, in the way he knew she needed taking care of.

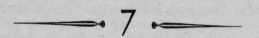

7

"DIDN'T THINK FOR a minute there." Charlie's voice came from an enormous distance. "You want me to help carry the gear into the house?"

"Thanks, Charlie, but it'll all wait until morning."

"Well. Sleep tight, then."

Sonia half heard Charlie's exaggerated yawn, then the door opening next to her ear. "Come on, little one," coaxed Craig's soft whisper.

Sleepily, Sonia opened her heavy eyes, and was immediately enfolded in strong arms pulling her out of the car. It was the same as sleep, that dark, still world. Her feet touched ground, but her head simply wanted to lie in that curve of his shoulder. "I didn't really fall asleep. I'm just resting for a minute," she murmured.

She heard his chuckle but didn't pay any attention. Winding her arms around his waist, she nuzzled her head under his chin and closed her eyes again.

In her dream, she was in motion, cradled close and moving through darkness. Lips pressed on her forehead, warm and smooth, once, and then again. The swaying motion didn't stop until her back sank onto a firm, cool surface. She was alone, bereft. Sliding sounds came from somewhere, then muted snaps, then...a zipper?...from a million miles away.

She forced her heavy eyes open, but that seemed to be part of the dream as well, because Craig was bending over her in that darkness, naked, his skin white in the

74

moonlight. Only he couldn't possibly be naked; they were still driving home.

Always, once Sonia had fallen asleep, she slept as if drugged, waking only slowly and with reluctance. Half smiling, Craig gently grazed her breasts with his knuckles, as one finger searched her camisole for a tiny pin. He found the pin and undid it, then silently pulled at the satin ribbons that held the camisole together. Her breasts strained free, all warm and heavy, pearl smooth.

He sank down to the bed, leaning over her, his hands gently chasing up the material until the satiny flesh was freed for him. In slow, silent motion, his lips dipped down and rubbed velvet-soft kisses in that warm pocket between her breasts. She stirred restlessly. "Don't wake," he murmured soothingly. "Don't wake, honey."

He ached from just that touch of her. She stirred again as he pulled off the camisole. "Craig?"

"Everything's fine," he whispered, and heard a rush of a sigh escape her lungs. He had to lift her hips a little to slide down the skirt. Her panties were little wisps of silk, so fragile; his hands glided them down over long thighs and slim calves.

"Cold," Sonia murmured.

He dropped the panties over the side of the bed, and when he turned back to her, she had rolled to her side, one leg bent at the knee, her arm unconsciously reaching for the empty spot on his side of the bed.

He didn't move for a moment. Didn't move, didn't breathe, didn't think. He didn't want to wake her. And he didn't want to stop looking. Moonlight rubbed silver on her bare skin; his lover was sprawled wanton in innocence, lovely in vulnerability.

She couldn't possibly know how much he loved her.

His heart ached with it; his head ached with it. His body, so aroused he felt on fire, burned with it. No one could ever understand what he'd felt when that slimy blond bastard had attacked her in Chicago. The explosive rage that anyone would dare hurt her . . . the splintering

frustration that he couldn't stop them . . . the searing guilt
that he had been responsible . . . his failure as a man to
protect his woman.

Somewhere, a long time back, he'd almost been
amused at how hard love had hit him. For Sonia, he'd
wanted to run rapids, climb mountains, battle foes, slay
dragons.

Obviously, there were no dragons, and Craig had never
considered himself a romantic man. He was a realist, a
man of action, no poet. And in the darkness he reached
for her, his touch so tender that at first she barely wakened.

Something smooth and warm and as light as a whisper
brushed on the soles of her feet, then her ankles and
calves. The very lightest pressure increased up the long
expanse of her thighs. Lips trailed farther, furrowing
sensual roads over the soft white flesh of her bottom, to
the base of her spine and up her vertebrae, one by one.
All nine million vertebrae. Fingers combed into her hair,
followed by more kisses, and then the trail started down
again.

Sonia stretched, murmuring sleepily. The lap of a
tongue feathered down all those vertebrae again, such
soft, secret licks that she felt all warm inside, warm and
cuddly and sleepy. The faint dampness traced the curve
of her hip with an intimacy that far surpassed any fantasy
or any dream.

Her lashes fluttered open, to a room that was dark.
Pitch dark. Though the moon was full in the windows,
her eyes could not adjust that quickly. And before they'd
had that chance, fingers splayed on her thighs, gently
urging her back flat to the mattress. Like a whisper of
promise, she felt lips stealing down on hers, soft, elusive . . . and with all the taste and familiar warmth of
Craig. Lazily, her arms lifted to snare her thief in the
night, but his head had already moved down.

His cheek was beard-roughened, buried between her
breasts. His hands cupped her breasts, and that stubbly

cheek grazed against them, the tender nuzzle of a lover, his breath warm on her bare skin. Roused from sleep, Sonia felt her breath caught somewhere between the dream and the reality. Her nipples tightened and swelled for his tongue, so warm-wet, so unbearably tender. A callused fingertip gently played with the tips, then his tongue again, then his fingertips. He hurt her. Really, he was hurting her terribly; the sweet, precious ache was both conscious and unconscious, spreading through all of her, engulfing her with intolerable longing.

"Easy," he whispered.

"Craig—"

His mouth sealed hers in a silent, soft kiss that disarmed with its gentleness. Teeth gently pulled at her lips; she parted them. A firm, smooth tongue immediately took advantage, assaulting hers in a tender, soft battle of tastes and textures and exploding senses.

Her lungs hauled in air when his lips finally lifted. Blackness had lightened to charcoal; the only color in that chiaroscuro was the liquid blue of his eyes, more intense, more heated, than she'd ever seen them before.

"Lie there," he whispered fiercely.

Lie there? She hadn't the strength of a kitten. Long, sinewed arms cuddled her up; she felt all the hypnotizing massage of lips and fingertips trailing down. Her breasts first, but then he switched to the inside of her forearm, her elbow, her ribs—parts of her body that had never felt like erogenous zones. They did now.

From sleep to sheer wanton insanity was a miraculous transition. She'd made love with Craig a thousand times and never felt the lustful awareness of her own flesh that her lover was now engraining, inch by inch, so slowly. Her hands reached out, her fingers raking through his hair, wanting to draw his face up to hers, his lips up to hers again. A most familiar heat was pressing against her abdomen, then her thigh. Craig was in motion, and the feel of his arousal ignited restless fires in her bloodstream. He wanted her. He *wanted* her!

She wanted him. Now! Her fingers curled over firm,
hot, smooth flesh—his hand covered hers, drew her away
from his thighs. Her leg rose to encircle him, to draw
him intimately closer, and another hand smoothed down
her thigh in a caress, stopping her. The man was an
expert at frustrating her.

So was the lover. His fingertips rushed over smooth
skin that receded beneath his palms, arched for his touch.
His tongue followed his fingertips, laving her breasts
again, trailing to her navel, shifting down to the ticklish,
curling hair below.

She shifted in a tangle of limbs and hands and lips,
a flush tainting her skin that only the moonlight could
see. "No," she murmured. A certain kind of touch and
she always turned shy.

"This time," he whispered back. "Easy. Easy, little
one . . ."

Inhibitions had no part in her relationship with Craig;
they never had. It wasn't inhibitions that lessened the
pleasure of a certain touch, but an inexplicable loneliness
at one being pleased and not the other. She wanted her
mate inside her, safe, warm, *with* her. She didn't like
alone. Her pleasure was irretrievably linked with his,
and her fingers reached again for the firm, hard evidence
of exactly how much he wanted her.

He brushed her seeking fingertips aside and bent lower,
his hands parting her thighs. Her muscles convulsed in
sudden, unwilling tension. Craig surged back up the length
of her to press a kiss on her lips. A long, lazy, slow
kiss, sensual . . . scolding her for that brief denial of her
response.

He was most unreasonable, her lover. She gave in,
offering him exactly the response he wanted, her flesh
brazenly arching for him again. Only then did his lips
leave hers and wander down.

His tongue slowly traced soft, private skin; his palms
pressed against the insides of her thighs. She surged up
for him, an angry rush of a sigh escaping her lungs. She

couldn't fight both him and herself, not in this delicious war.

Her skin grew damp and hot and pliable under his hands, his tongue; in a sweet, warm rush she dissolved for him, crying out in the darkness. And again, yet again... Spun crystals exploded behind her eyes, and moments later she clung to him, exhausted, exhilarated, unbearably replete. And yet lonely...

Craig gently pushed back her dampened hair, his touch soothing her until her heartbeat again quieted. "You are my incredibly beautiful lady," he murmured.

She had the terrible urge to bury her face in his shoulder in shyness. "No."

His lips brushed her cheek. "Yes. So responsive. So lovely. So special," he said softly. "And your body always gives me this foolish little argument when I want to love you a certain way. It's sheer pleasure for me just to watch you, little one, don't you know that? I'm here; I'm with you... There's nothing wrong, Sonia."

"I never thought anything we did was wrong," she whispered back, and sighed, her eyes closing as she snuggled against his chest. "Craig?"

"Hmm?" He pulled the sheet up to her chin, then slid lower to curl more closely around her.

"You're a very special man," she remarked.

His lips curled in a smile.

She reached up, sharing a kiss of smiles before curling close to him again. Her eyes closed. Her mind was in a desultory pre-sleep haze after being so very thoroughly loved. Lingering sensations of pleasure floated all around her, not just from his lovemaking but from now simply being held and stroked before she fell asleep.

Part of that sleepy euphoria was the intimate feel of his hardness against her abdomen. It was his turn, she thought groggily, and fought to stay awake. Her hand reached out to caress him.

His hand laced loosely into hers and tucked it in a warm, secure embrace... and she fell asleep.

* * *

Squinting, Sonia bent forward until her face was an inch from the bathroom mirror. *There.* Right there at the outside corner of her eye. A wrinkle was definitely settling in. Particularly when she squinted with that determined expression.

When you were worried about finding flaws, it was amazing how fast they all jumped at you. One sunburned nose, one cracked toenail, knobby knees... and when Sonia turned around and held a hand mirror to the light, she saw a single white hair in the middle of her crown. Her fingers raced to pluck it out.

She lost it.

Wiggling her towel-clad bottom, she frantically combed through the curls on her crown again. The damn thing was elusive, but she knew it was there. She plucked the nasty thing, wincing.

"Sonia?" Two sharp raps echoed on the bathroom door. "You're actually up? You still want to go for a ride this morning?"

"Just give me five minutes," Sonia sang out, her cheerfulness volubly denying that it was unusual for her to be up at six in the morning. Actually, she'd been awake since five. Worrying.

At the speed of sound, she rushed back to the bedroom, drew on old pink jeans with a pastel plaid blouse, riding boots, and belt, and then lingered another few seconds in front of the dresser mirror. She would not have been surprised to see some drastic signs of deterioration. A single white hair didn't count.

The last she knew, her husband had been attracted to her—wildly so. Nothing had *seemed* wrong between the two of them even yesterday. Nothing had *seemed* wrong in a month. And there was nothing drastically unusual if a husband and wife didn't share equal pleasure during a single night's encounter. For heaven's sake, it couldn't always be even-Steven. The next night simply made up for that. It was part of a marriage, a give and take.

Always, Craig had been an inventive, giving, passionate lover...maybe with a slight inclination toward insatiability. Since he'd built up that same slight inclination in her, they'd just never had a problem. Well. Some slight problems *controlling* themselves occasionally...

Sonia chewed absently on her lip, staring at the mirror, and then hurried from the room. Last night...Her cheeks flushed as she waved a good morning to Charlie in the kitchen and headed out the back door. Last night her husband had proved to be a most tender, erotic lover, forcing unexpectedly uninhibited responses from her, all but demanding the most incredible, intense pleasure...

And yet he hadn't taken his own. Craig had never been a selfish lover, but after more than a month Sonia had been frankly expecting...a quickie. A rather explosive quickie. Followed by long, leisurely "seconds." Sonia knew her lover quite well. *Abstinence* was not in his vocabulary; he'd probably never even heard the word, and she suddenly saw that for a month he'd been...different. Very small things, really. The P.I.'s receipt he'd kept from her, the occasional withdrawn look in his eyes, the way he'd all but handcuffed her to his side at work...

You're making far too much of it, she chided herself as she strode outside. In the distance, she could see the two Andalusians pawing the ground. Craig was holding them by the reins, murmuring to them with his back to her. He wore old jeans that fit snugly around his hips, and his checked shirt rippled over his shoulders as he moved. The look of the man was downright erotic even in the broad light of day. When he turned to her, his smile would have aroused sexual feelings in a nun.

You're making too much of it, she repeated to herself, and acknowledged wryly that she would undoubtedly continue to make too much of it. She hadn't been able to shut off her intuition since five this morning. She had great plans for growing old with this man, and she knew darn well that a single white hair and one pending wrinkle weren't about to turn him off, but something, dammit, was wrong.

Mostly in play, but partly to test his response, she sassily patted his fanny on the way to being offered a leg up.

As if to assure her everything was absolutely normal, he then forced her to lean down from her horse to accept a kiss. "You sleep all right?" he asked.

She shook her head. "Someone woke me up in the middle of the night," she announced.

"No kidding?"

"You wouldn't believe what he did to me."

Belle snorted impatiently. Craig ignored the mare, grasping the reins with one hand as his free palm roamed over Sonia's thigh and ribs, undoubtedly checking for signs of injury. "You don't seem any the worse for wear. What happened?"

Such innocence, such big blue eyes filled with innocence...and such a lusty smile. Sonia, there isn't a damn thing wrong with anything, she told herself. "Just a pirate in the night," she mentioned blithely. "He took my virtue but left the jewels. Not to worry."

"What virtue?"

She leaned over her horse's mane. "The same virtue I had plenty of, Mr. Hamilton, until I met you. Now, are you going to continue to tease me in front of this yard full of ranch hands, or are we going to have a dead race for the hills?"

Belle snorted noisily, her choice obvious. Both Black Lightning and Sonia's Belle had become used to their morning ride.

"I would prefer to tease you," Craig said lazily as he put his foot in the stirrup. "For that matter," he added gravely, "your cheeks look windburned, honey. I'd advise you to force your pirate to shave next time. And I certainly hope that no other portion of your body has that same reddish—"

It took a great deal to make Sonia color. To the sound of his low laughter, her thighs pressed tight against her mare's flanks, and in seconds the wind was whipping through her hair. "Two bits says I'll beat you," she called over her shoulder.

Belle was bursting with energy, all power and grace beneath her, responsive to her suddenly ebullient mood and the wonderfully cool morning and the path they both knew so well.

Belle was responsive . . . but not as fast as Craig's Black Lightning. It hardly mattered, since she knew Craig would let her win. In moments, he was beside her, matching her pace with his own, his hair whipped back sleek by the wind, his shirt flattened against his tautly muscled chest.

The long green slopes fell behind them, until their house and the ranch buildings became small dots on a distant landscape and the river looked like a silver fluorescent rope in the sunlight. They didn't slow the horses until the trail started to climb and twist. They were both out of breath by then, ready for quieter sport.

The southwestern corner of the ranch was more arid than the rest. They inevitably rode toward those acres. The verdant green and gentle roll of the major portion of the ranch was nature's gift, where cattle or horses could graze and the land held a richness of water and trees in the foothills. Not here.

Some would have called this a wasteland, where pockets of wind had found a home for centuries and erosion had taken its toll. Here, there was oil beneath the stubborn rock, oil Craig had tapped when he was seventeen to secure his heritage, but no one traversed the land now except the two of them. Through a narrow canyon, the trail wandered south, and suddenly they rode high up along a ridge. A stark gulch beneath them reflected myriad strata of blue and green and yellow in the sunlit rock. Wildflowers stubbornly insisted on growing, tucked in crevices here and here. The beauty was in the wildness, in the stretch of endless sky and space and loneliness.

An eagle soared overhead, undoubtedly searching for a very foolish rabbit for its breakfast. Sonia exchanged smiles with Craig. It was always a good omen when they spotted an eagle. They watched it soar and dip and then wing off with a mournful scream of frustration.

"We haven't camped out here in a long time," Craig said idly.

"Too long," Sonia agreed, as she stroked her mare's sleek neck.

"I think I could stay here forever."

Sonia smiled. "And instead you'll undoubtedly work late again today," she teased, knowing full well that as important as his land was to Craig, it alone could never keep him satisfied.

"In another week, I hope the long hours will be over. You have plans for the day, honey?"

She nodded absently. "Nothing hard and set, but I thought I'd head into town." She cocked her head with a wry smile. "Do you realize I've barely been off the ranch since we got home? Once to go to work with you, and once for my parents' party. Lazy is one thing, but this is ridiculous! Charlie's even taken to doing the grocery shopping. I think," she added conspiratorially, "that he must have a girl in town."

She glanced at Craig, expecting him to share the humor of Charlie's unwonted domestic role, and instead found him staring straight ahead, an oddly tense pulse working in his throat. "Craig?"

He turned to her, his smile so determinedly casual that she relaxed again. "What time do you plan to go into town?" he asked.

She shrugged. "I don't know. After lunch, probably. I thought I'd see Marina, window-shop . . . well. I have every intention of spending a *little* of your money . . ." She still couldn't seem to raise an honest smile. Perplexed, she stared at him.

"Sonia, are you bored?" he asked quietly.

"No, of course not. I've never in my life been bored."
She sighed, and with a flick of the reins turned her mare
toward home. "It's just been so long since we've *really*
been home," she admitted softly. "You're into the project
full time now. I knew that was coming, but I worked
with you more before, especially in Washington. There
isn't a darn thing I can do to help you now..."

"You've helped every damned step of the way," he
said roughly. When she glanced at him, his voice gentled.
"I can more than understand that you'd want time to
explore your own...thing. There is time, now, Sonia,
and if you really want to work for Marina—"

"Craig, do you want a baby?" Sonia tugged on the
reins, slowing Belle to a halt.

Craig stopped, too, studying his wife, picturing her
first with a burgeoning tummy and then with a baby in
her arms. Both images roused instant loving, protective
instincts. Fiercely, he wanted her to bear his child, a
child with her loving nature and their blend of strengths
and all that *future* that a baby implied. He wanted her
daughter.

He'd settle for her son. And he'd waited a long time
for her to ask that soft-spoken question.

But not now.

Sonia didn't know how his feelings had changed since
that incident in Chicago, and he didn't want her to. The
issues were between him and himself, things he had to
work out on his own.

A man protected his woman. An archaic instinct, really;
machismo was out this decade. Unfortunately, it was
engrained in him to the core. At gut level, he had failed
her.

Sonia was more fragile than rose petals. She was
gregarious and sassy and innately trusting; love bubbled
from her as from a never-ending well. He'd risked all of
that, in Chicago. A man who'd failed to protect his
lady...How could he protect a child?

"Craig?" Sonia was looking at him curiously.

"Do *you* want a child?" he asked quietly.

Her eyes softened. "When you do."

He didn't want either, at the moment. Not a child, and not her working where she was exposed to the public. He wanted her *safe*. "I want you happy," he said simply, and stared straight ahead. "Look, see Marina if you want to. Then we'll talk about it."

He could feel her confusion; his eyes narrowed deliberately on the stretch of trail ahead. "Listen, lady. I'm about to reclaim my fifty cents. You've got to the start of ten to get that lazy mare in motion."

"*Lazy!*" Her thighs instantly pressed tightly to Belle, both horse and rider offended at the insult.

Craig trailed her laughter down through the hills, savoring it, cherishing it, his mood lifting with it.

He was going to let her win again. Halfway down the trail, he slowed up long enough to dig a hand in his pocket and make sure he had the dollar she was certain to demand. Sonia was a stickler for paying one's debts.

So was Craig.

8

SONIA'S EYEBROWS LIFTED in surprise as she neared her
little Rabbit. George was standing next to it. He was
nearly as much of an institution around Craig's ranch as
Charlie was; he was the best of ranch hands and had
been with Craig for years.

He was also about the size of a fairy-tale giant, his
leathery skin permanently sun weathered and his blunt
shoulders rather hunched as he stood with hat in hand.
"I was wondering if I could get a ride to town, ma'am,"
he said politely.

Her eyebrows rose just a fraction farther. "Well, of
course you can, George, but..." She had to raise her
chin to see his eyes. The man had to be six feet fifty.
And was looking oddly uncomfortable. "The trucks all
break down at once on you?" she questioned teasingly.
George had never asked for a lift to town before, and
the kind of supplies he usually brought back would hardly
fit in her Rabbit.

"Sort of." He shifted. "I need some parts from town.
Just thought if you were going, you might not mind if I
tagged along."

"Of course I don't mind," she assured him, and slid
into the driver's seat, motioning George to get in as well.
It was like watching a bear climb into a bassinet, but he
managed to cram his long body into the passenger seat,
his knees just about touching his chin. He stared politely
ahead as she started the engine. "If it would save you a

trip, I'd be happy to buy those parts for you," Sonia offered.

"That's okay, ma'am," he said flatly.

Which just about settled that; George never wasted words. Sonia repressed a chuckle. One *did* get the feeling he would be more comfortable on a horse than next to her in the Rabbit. Charlie had driven to town in one of the pickups, she remembered fleetingly; perhaps the other was in use as well and George had simply been stuck for a ride. She glanced absently in the rearview mirror. Her pert white sharkskin skirt, soft purple blouse, and sandals didn't blend too well with her companion's rough jeans and spurred boots. It didn't bother her, but poor George was radiating nervousness.

"Tell me where you need to go," Sonia suggested lightly. "Lawson's or the hardware? My business won't take long, George; if you need to get something quickly back to the ranch I could cut it out altogether. For that matter—"

"I just want to go to Brock's, ma'am."

Brock's. Marina's department store. Sonia adjusted the sun visor and managed to hide her surprise. George must be buying something for a girl friend; no wonder he was so untalkative. She spent the next five miles whimsically envisioning a romance in the offing.

The thought delighted her, but... well. George wasn't exactly handsome. He was true-blue loyal, dependable, and strong-hearted, but his speech was usually rather crusty—when he got around to talking. He spent at least four nights a week with a bottle and four poker buddies; he occasionally liked a good brawl, and... he chewed.

Sonia was hard pressed to imagine the kind of woman he would shop at Brock's for. *George?* And on ranch time, in the middle of the working day? It *had* to be love. George was the type who would come to work with pneumonia; playing hooky wasn't his thing at all.

She cleared her throat as they neared the edge of town. "You know, George, if I could help you out by buying something for you," she repeated.

"No, thank you, ma'am."

The "ma'am" drove her nuts, but she let it be.

George needed a shower. Not drastically, but Sonia rolled down the window just a little instead of opting for air conditioning. Wedding plans filled her mind . . . difficult to imagine, though, because the giant next to her didn't exude the most romantic of auras. Still, she wanted to help him.

"You're looking for a special gift?" she tried tactfully.

George shifted uneasily. "Just parts, ma'am."

Parts. In Marina's store. All right. Sonia parked on the street in Cold Creek, and almost before she'd put the key in her purse found George opening her door for her. She blinked, stared at him in total bewilderment as she stepped out of the car. The last she knew, she could open a door on her own, and chivalry wasn't exactly the first word that came to mind in free-associating George's name.

The town had boomed in the last few years. Stores and businesses had popped up; the library was new, and suddenly parking was at a premium. Cold Creek had never heard of McDonald's ten years before; now there were two . . . and enough traffic to justify them. Sonia had mixed feelings about some of the changes. She was afraid the town would lose its sleepy western flavor, but overall it was hard to find fault with growth that brought in jobs and prosperity for her neighbors.

She started walking with George at her side. His legs were miles long, and he was doing a touching job of trying to slow down to her pace. She tried to speed up accordingly; he tried to slow his gait further.

Laurel and Hardy, she thought wryly. Relief filled her as they finally reached the display windows of Brock's. George awkwardly rushed forward to open the glass doors. "Thank you," she murmured. It was like being trailed by an apprentice knight in shining armor, give or take the plug of Redman tobacco in his cheek.

Counters laden with cosmetics and lingerie confronted them; George stopped stock still, his expression not unlike that of a calf being led to a pen. Sonia chuckled;

she couldn't help it. "I had in mind going to see someone in the back offices," she said lightly. "I'll be there half an hour or so. Will that be long enough for you to get your ... er ... parts?"

"You're not leaving the store, ma'am?"

She bit her lip to keep from chuckling. "George, if I can buy something for you so you won't have to go through all this—"

George looked blank.

Sonia gave up. "I'll see you in a few ..." She'd taken a step forward; so did George—directly on her heels. How could a man so graceful on a horse be such a clumsy puppy in a mere department store? She sighed. "I'll meet you at the front door in half an hour. All right?"

"Sure, ma'am."

But he certainly looked uneasy. Sonia swallowed a grin as she wended her way past the display of shoes and then summer clothing. Marina's offices were in back, past a steel door that led to a sudden confusion of type-writers and phones and bustle, a total contrast to the carpeted retreat Marina had tried to make of the store itself.

Sonia paused in the doorway to her friend's office. Marina had a phone to her ear and her glasses perched on her cinnamon-colored hair. Her brown linen dress had clearly been through a rough morning, wisps of her hair were going every which way, and in usual style, she'd bitten off her lipstick. The desk was stacked high; some-where in the debris were a computer terminal and type-writer. Marina inevitably looked buried. She was only five feet tall, and at forty-five had a few well-earned wrinkles on her brow, bright blue eyes that radiated shrewd intelligence, and a broad, warm smile the minute she noticed Sonia in the doorway.

"Call you back," she barked into the phone, and waved Sonia over. "Get in here, you hermit. You haven't been to see me in ages. I want to know what you think of these."

In minutes, Sonia was surrounded by fabric swatches and samples. Marina shoved a chair against the backs of Sonia's legs and thrust a cup of jet-black, overstrong coffee into her hand.

"I've *got* to make some decisions on next spring's line," Marina said distractedly. "It's everything I've already talked to you about, Sonia. I made a fortune on dressy clothes in the past, but that's just not what's required anymore. Many of the women who shop here nowadays are holding down new jobs and buying professional-looking clothing at reasonable prices. Now, I want to make some changes, but I don't want to lower the quality of our merchandise. I won't carry cheap lines, of course. Workmanship and taste are still crucial, but..."

They talked about the prime rate, Sonia's roses, Marina's cats, and local politics, and between times scribbled out choices of style and compared notes. Marina's life was the store. Sonia loved the chatter and always had. Clothes had once been her business; she loved the feel and smell and look of fabrics; she loved to work with color and had an intrinsic understanding of the way a style could affect a woman's mood and confidence.

"You've been thinking about the job, haven't you?" Marina probed.

"About working with you as a fashion consultant?" Sonia's voice was thoughtful. "You know I'd like to, Marina, but the issue is time. We're finally home for a long period now, but Craig's busier than ever on the extraction project. I could do some of the ranch paperwork for him; I like being free to take off with him when he has to travel, and..." She hesitated, finally deciding not to mention that she wanted a child to be part of her future as well.

"Perhaps you could work here part time, then, Sonia." Marina had that determined set to her jaw. "Look, I can't tell you how many women ask for help. They come in knowing just how much they want to spend, but they don't have the vaguest idea what clothes to choose. Suddenly, we've got jobs for women in this area. Only they haven't gotten out of jeans in a century. Now they need comfortable, reasonable, attractive outfits to wear to work, and I want them to feel comfortable walking in here—"

"And spending their money—"

"Oh, hush, you."

"On clothes that make them feel good about themselves."

"Now you're talking."

"You have a buyer," Sonia reminded her.

"And she's terrific at selecting quality stuff in up-to-date styles, but she doesn't *know* the women in this area; she doesn't understand the kind of jobs they have; and she can't talk to them the way you do."

"Lord, you must be desperate for cheap help," Sonia said wryly, and they both laughed. They talked a few more minutes before Sonia gave Marina a quick hug and told her she'd get back to her in a few days. She stepped out of the office, humming under her breath, energy restlessly surging through her after sitting so long. Pushing open the steel door that led to the selling floor, she took a step through and nearly collided with George.

He didn't, she noticed with surprise, have any packages in his hands. In fact, he didn't look as if he'd moved a fraction of an inch from where she'd left him. An odd gleam of wariness suddenly flickered in her eyes, then was gone.

"Ready to go, ma'am?" he questioned politely.

"Actually . . ." She glanced up at him. "Did you finish your . . . shopping?"

He opened his mouth and then took a nervous breath. "If you have anything else to do, Mrs. Hamilton, I got no problems waiting around."

Which didn't answer her question, Sonia noticed. "I have one more thing I'd like to do, George, if you'll give me another fifteen minutes. You could catch a quick cup of coffee in Harry's across the street, couldn't—"

"That's okay, ma'am."

Actually, it wasn't. Sonia determinedly caught those eyes shifting hurriedly away from hers. "I have just a small amount of *personal* shopping I need to do," she said gently.

"That's okay, too, ma'am."

"George..." A wisp of a smile touched her soft lips. She'd planned the trip to town for one main purpose, and as much as she loved Marina, talking clothes wasn't it. Pleasing Craig was her purpose, and though George's unprecedented behavior was amusing, Sonia hadn't really planned on shopping with a sidekick who stuck to her like glue. "I really think you'd be more comfortable waiting in the car," she tried one more time.

He evidently didn't think so, standing silently before her with his hat in his hands. I'm sorry, George, she thought briefly, and swept into the lingerie department, hearing a booted foot abruptly stumble behind her.

If George wanted to watch her shop for bras and panties, it was certainly fine with her. The plans she had in mind for Craig that evening, though, were rather private. Totally private, actually. Slowly she fingered a beige satin nightgown on a mannequin and turned with a deliberate smile for George. "What do you think?"

He opened his mouth, then closed it, his cheeks turning beet red, and his hands twisting his hat. "Pardon, ma'am?"

The counter next to the nightgowns was piled with bras, lovely filmy little see-through things. She lifted one rose-colored confection to the light and again turned to George with a cheerful smile. "I don't know whether I like this or the blue one..."

He fled.

He stationed himself near the door and turned toward an innocuous display of scarves and belts. Poor George, Sonia thought, but the dancing light in her eyes had already died. A thoughtful expression replaced it. There were days when it took a bulldozer to get through to her.

She suddenly realized that George hadn't accompanied her to Brock's to get parts, and he hadn't come to get a present for his girl friend, either.

He was here, she realized, to watch over her. Amusement warred with exasperation inside her. *Craig, you silly, foolish man. Dammit, I'm all right. When are you going to get that through your head?*

"Would you like some help, Mrs. Hamilton?" A soft-eyed blonde stepped shyly forward.

"No, thank you, Sharon."

With a ruthless eye, Sonia fingered only the most luxurious of satins, the most frivolous of laces. It was time she took some direct action against her increasingly enigmatic husband. Craig could occasionally be unbudgeable. Bullheaded, in short. Maybe it was going to take him a little more time to get that incident in Chicago out of his head, and maybe the wisest thing for her to do was simply ignore that receipt she'd found in his desk, ignore George, ignore all the little signs that her husband's possessiveness had burgeoned out of control.

Patience, she urged herself. In all but one arena. She held a lacy shocking-pink robe up to the light and put it down again. Not nearly sexy enough.

Craig had always been a strong, dominating personality. It might be a well-kept secret most of the time, but she was a long way from being a marshmallow herself. And not that she really believed anything was seriously wrong with their relationship, but occasionally it couldn't hurt to use a little guerrilla warfare. Her eyes lit up and narrowed on an emerald satin nightgown.

Now *there* was lethal ammunition.

Sonia stretched lazily as she stood up from the table. "I can't understand why I'm so sleepy. Think I'll turn in early tonight."

Charlie lifted his eyes from the plate of cherry pie. "You look about as sleepy as popcorn that just got the heat. And it's only eight o'clock, you know."

"I know." One by one, she fed the dinner plates into the dishwasher, trying to work slower than her usual speed, which was like Parnelli Jones in a car race. Craig had called to say he would be working late, that he'd have dinner in town and hoped to be home by nine.

"And did you *know* that those pups of yours chewed straight through a brand-new harness last night?" Charlie asked.

"The harness shouldn't have been left on the ground," Sonia instantly defended them.

Charlie snorted. "That Rayburn lady in town said she'd take one on, and pay good money for it, too."

"She doesn't have any kids." After she made a swift swipe of the counter, the kitchen looked spotless—barring the broiler pan in the sink.

"So?"

"Charlie, I'm not going to sell the pups to just anybody."

"Take out the *just*," Charlie suggested. "Five bucks says you don't sell any of them to anybody, flat out." He shoved his plate forward and lit his cigar. Sonia could have kicked him. Instead, she scrubbed the broiler pan, washed his dessert plate, whipped the leftover pie into the refrigerator, and turned to face Charlie with another ostentatious yawn.

"What'd you buy in town?" he asked her, as if she hadn't given him every opportunity to amble toward the door.

"Nothing."

"You came home with a package."

"Did your mother ever tell you you were nosy?" She leaned back against the counter, regarding her momentary nemesis with an affectionate grin. "Do you hear me asking what *you* did in town all day?"

"I went to the bank, the hardware store, had lunch with Jim Olsen, and checked out the colt Baker wants to sell. Now, what was in the package?"

"Peanut butter."

"Five bucks says it's got a neckline that'll make Craig holler."

"Craig doesn't *holler.*"

Charlie snorted. "Just 'cause he doesn't yell at you, I wouldn't be making no rash assumptions that man can't let loose with the best of them. You just got him hoodwinked so he thinks you're softer than melted butter."

She had a fine answer for him, but unfortunately the phone rang. Charlie had only to raise a hand to reach the wall extension. Adjusting his cigar, he barked into the phone, "Hamiltons', Charlie here."

His face changed from teasing, gregarious Charlie to an odd stillness. "It's all right. You can talk to me; I'll relay the message. Yes . . ."

She was watching him curiously when his eyes darted in her direction, then shifted. Nothing important, he mouthed to her with a smile, then stood up from the chair, taking the phone as far away as its cord would let him.

"You know, Mr. Hamilton was expecting a little more action by now. As in, results. Not that I'm saying you don't know your business, but if I were you . . ."

His voice was low, and he had turned his face away from her. Sonia felt something twist inside her. Maybe the person on the other end of the line wasn't the Chicago detective Craig had hired to find the muggers; maybe the call was just business. Like hell.

Charlie hung up a moment later, and crushed his cigar in the ashtray on the counter. "Craig told some dude he might be interested in some horses of his," he said blithely.

"Sure." Sonia straightened from the counter and headed for the door, her tone suddenly crisp. "Did I tell you George went to Brock's with me this afternoon, Charlie? He bought a fan belt for the pickup."

"He wha—?" Charlie's voice trailed off. He stared at her, guilty awareness imprinted on his face as clearly as a milk mustache. "Now, look. Sonia . . ."

"Forget it." She kissed his cheek. "Sleep well."

Enough, she told herself firmly. Enough, enough, enough. Everyone on the ranch seemed to be involved in conspiracies, primarily regarding her. Since when had anyone ever had to treat her like porcelain?

In her bathroom, she flicked on the tub faucets and reached for a vial of perfume. She poured in a few drops and, on second thought, emptied the little bottle. The fragrance burst free in the steamy water; she stole one more look at the clock in the bedroom, then closed the doors to seal in the scent, and rapidly stripped off her clothes. Eight twenty-four. She had half an hour, anyway, before Craig was due home.

Her planned soak was a quick one, just long enough for the perfume to permeate her skin. From there she stepped out to wrap a towel around herself, applied a scented cream to her feet and hands and throat, and when that was dry dropped the towel and hurried into the bedroom. Lights, she thought absently, and promptly turned on the shaded lamp on the dresser, then closed the curtains with a single glance outside to make sure Craig wasn't driving in at that instant.

He wasn't. The green satin nightgown was hidden in the closet; gently, she pulled it off the hanger and slipped it over her head. In front of the dresser mirror, she adjusted the two tiny straps and took a first glance.

The gown definitely had Garbo seductiveness, the satin slinky from neckline to floor, flowing smoothly even as it outlined her breasts and tummy and thighs. In its center was an embroidered cutout, baring a triangle of white skin at her navel. Her mood lifted into irrepressible wickedness as she brushed her hair into a deliberately disheveled mass of curls. No lipstick, but she bit her lips three times and then stared again. She *definitely* liked that little peephole in the center of the gown.

Glancing at the clock again, she hastily pawed through the trinkets in a box on her dresser. You're *not* going to do this, she told herself, even as she drew out a tiny round glass jewel. Her father had given her the necklace when she was a little girl; it wasn't valuable; she'd broken the chain years ago and simply kept the little green bit of glass because she loved it. It fit, precisely, in her navel.

She glanced at the mirror again. For *heaven's sake*, take that *out of there*. This is not Arabia. She performed a tentative seductive undulation with her tummy; the stone popped out. Cheeks flushed, she picked it up, and gave the clock another worried look.

Ten to nine. And she'd forgotten the wine. With the glass jewel in her hand, she rushed back to the kitchen, grabbed a tray and two glasses, then added a bottle of wine to it. She started for the bedroom again, then rushed back for the corkscrew.

She was out of breath by the time the clock said nine, ready to collapse on the bed, exhausted. Listening for the sound of Craig's car, she opened the wine, poured a glass to set on his nightstand, then poured one for herself. Moments later, she lay back against the pillows, carefully arranged the emerald satin gown around her, stubbornly stuck the jewel back in her navel, and reached for her wine.

After a first sip, she rearranged the straps on the gown. The satin plunged as it was, but every little bit helped.

By the third sip, she relaxed and stopped panting like a mad thing. One couldn't race around like a whirlwind and then instantly feel seductive, navel jewel or no navel jewel.

She set down the glass and closed her eyes. Truthfully, it was just as well Craig wasn't here at this specific moment, because she just didn't feel all that seductive. She felt . . . confused.

George had been . . . funny. Charlie's face when he was fibbing over that phone call had also been funny. But her sense of humor seemed to have temporarily deserted her. She felt oddly disturbed, not able to pinpoint any exact source of worry, but just feeling it, as she'd felt after Craig's one-sided lovemaking the night before.

As far as George and the investigator went, she knew Craig was acting out of love for her. He wanted to care for her and protect her and ensure that nothing like the Chicago incident ever happened to her again.

For that, she loved him.

But for the moment, all of it was just bringing back to the forefront of her mind the incident she'd been trying so hard to forget. She couldn't possibly live her life looking over her shoulder for someone to attack her; she didn't want to and she wouldn't. She'd worked it all through weeks ago. Crime was real; insane people who liked to hurt others were real...The attack had shaken her world. And for the first week, she *had* been looking over her shoulder...but no more. The door was locked at night now, but she wasn't going to stop smiling at the gas-station attendant just because she didn't really know him all that well; she wasn't about to avoid going anywhere out of fear. She refused to live that way; she refused to be afraid any longer...

She opened her eyes and glanced at the clock again. Ten. A creak sounded from the living room, and she jumped. Darn it, it was just a night sound; she knew that.

Craig, would you kindly come home and make love to me? she thought irritably. You have no idea how fast that kind of nonsensical reaction would disappear if *you*, my overprotective husband, would put the whole thing out of *your* mind as well.

The clock edged toward ten-fifteen, and still there was only silence. Sonia took one last sip of wine and closed her eyes.

9

CRAIG WANDERED THROUGH the dark hall and paused in the doorway to their bedroom. The dresser lamp radiated faint yellow circles that did not quite reach the bed. Sonia was sleeping, her cheek nestled against the pillow with her palm beneath it. His eyes darkened just at the look of her.

She was lying on her side, uncovered but for the green gown, one knee bent forward, her free arm thrown back, her lips slightly parted. His brows narrowed fractionally as he noticed an odd, hard, glistening object on her stomach, and he tiptoed forward.

His lips twitched as he removed the green glass jewel from her navel. What if it had cut her? Silently, he placed the stone on the bedside table, then straightened to tug off his tie and shirt, his eyes still on his wife, glancing once at the glass of wine by his side of the bed.

A blind man could have figured out what the lady had in mind. Sonia was a little blind herself if she thought she needed any tricks to make him want her.

Tugging off the rest of his clothes, he flicked off the dresser lamp and came to her in the darkness. She didn't stir when he gently lifted her to curl back the covers and tuck her into them. He fitted her close against him, heard her groggy murmur of approval, and whispered to her firmly to go back to sleep.

She did.

But *he* couldn't. With her head in the cradle of his

shoulder and his arm around her, he stared hard and unseeing into the darkness, and after a time he reached for the glass of wine.

Later, even after he'd forced his eyes closed, he was conscious of her warm body folded against him, of the cool satin teasing the length of his flesh. The smell of her hair and skin, the weight of her breast so heavy and supple against his chest, the softness of her cheek . . .

The hush of silence was all around him, dark and empty. Lonely. His whole body throbbed with wanting her. Wearily, his eyes blinked open again. Sleep—real sleep—had eluded him for weeks. Tonight was going to be no different.

Men were chasing her. Hundreds of them, one with pale, light eyes that shone out of the darkness like steady pinpricks. She tripped and got up again, tripped and stumbled to her feet again, sobbing. She was wearing green, something bright and soft; it was tearing, ripping from her. "Don't you *touch* me!" she screamed. A hundred hands flashed in front of her eyes. Laughter. Their laughter.

She crashed into a tree; she turned around and tumbled over a bush. The laughter chased her through the fog, coming closer; the darkness was somehow green and she ached with terror, hating it, sick with it. Clawlike hands grabbed at her shoulder, twisting her, whirling her around. *"No! Get away from me—"*

"Honey. Wake up, love . . ."

She beat out with her fists, wild, smashing blows. She felt a palm on her stomach and exploded. "Leave him *alone*. You *leave him alone . . ."*

"Sonia."

Green faded to darkness; her eyes blinked open, disoriented. Her whole body was violently trembling but she instantly recognized the firm arms around her as Craig's.

"Easy, easy, love," he whispered. "It was only a dream.

You were dreaming, Sonia. You're here and safe. *Nothing* will harm you. Nothing. I promise you . . ."

"I . . ." For an instant, she couldn't seem to stop shaking; she couldn't even talk. She buried her face in the warm flesh of his chest, wrapped her arms around his waist, and just held on. So foolish. Already she knew how foolish it was to relive their attack in a dream; if she hadn't had it on her mind before she went to sleep . . .

Craig's hand stroked and soothed. His fingers brushed back her hair; his lips pressed on her forehead and cheeks, and then he just held her again. "Nothing's going to hurt you," he promised again, his voice so low it was almost a whisper. There was a discordant echo somewhere, something almost like anger emanating from him, but his touch could not have been more tender. "You're right here," he murmured. "Safe, little one. Completely safe."

She raised her face to his. "So . . . stupid," she whispered groggily. "So stupid. Craig, I *haven't* been dreaming about it." Her tongue was still thick with sleep, her mind still in that half-confusion of dreams, yet the words kept coming out in a helpless tumble. "I *haven't*. It was only this once. I've forgotten, completely forgotten, about what happened."

He shifted over her, his mouth pressing on hers, sealing the words back. He heard her and knew exactly what she wanted to tell him—and he believed her not at all. Sonia had forgotten nothing. Guilt lanced through him like a raging ache, the same ache that had haunted him for weeks . . . and his lips were rough on hers, smooth and hard and demanding. And then not. His guilt was not Sonia's. Suddenly, the only thing in his head was the need to drive those memories from Sonia's mind. Block them, erase them, obliterate them.

"Craig—"

He tossed back the sheets and heard her intake of breath as the cool night air trembled over her skin. His fingers pushed up the nightgown, his palms sliding up over thighs and hips and stomach far softer than satin.

"Craig. I—"

In a smooth swish, the nightgown landed on the floor. He stole the pillow from beneath her, and it landed on the floor as well. The firm surface of the mattress was all he wanted beneath her, a playground he knew well. In his head was everything he'd ever learned of Sonia, a thousand nights of touching behind them, a knowledge of everything that had ever pleased her, every special caress that had ever fired her passion.

She *would* forget the Chicago nightmare. His lips parted on hers, open, his tongue stealing inside like a swift thief; her warm sweetness was his treasure. He drew her arms up, holding them by the wrists, and felt her limbs twist around him, her breasts arching instinctively for the crush of his weight.

He calmed a little at her instant responsiveness. But only a little. He wanted more, much more, of her, and his lips rushed down her throat, down to her breasts. His mouth captured one honey-tipped nipple, not giving her a chance to breathe, a chance to think. He didn't want her to think. He wanted every memory exorcised, every thought buried.

He rolled over and shifted her on top of him, his hands sweeping down the slope of her spine, fingers splaying on the smooth flesh of her bottom, rubbing her deliberately against the cradle of his thighs, forcing her awareness of his arousal between them. *"Feel,"* he murmured. *"Feel* how much I want you. I'll take you so high you'll never come down. Never, Sonia."

So fierce. A delicious tremble rippled through her. A month of loneliness for the lover she knew Craig to be sent an explosion of sensual feelings to every nerve ending in her body. The dark night and stillness and hazy sleep-fog were all part of that. His rushing hands and breath and pounding heartbeat were so much more.

His lips were everywhere—on her fingertips, trailing along her arms, stealing down her sides. His tongue lapped the underside of her breasts, first one, then the other, and her fingers curled in his hair, pressing into the thick, dark mat, holding him to her. The breath hissed out of her lungs as his tongue went lower, yet that intimate touch was not his ultimate goal. His lips had miles to go, down the long slope of her thighs, then up her back. His teeth nipped at the soft flesh of her fanny, and she twisted.

Almost, a smile touched his features. She didn't like that. It wasn't quite...nice. He nipped again, asserting his control...a tender, gentle control. For this moment, her body belonged to him, every inch, every crevice, every hollow and swell. He molded her softness beneath his hands. He claimed her breath when he turned her, seeking her mouth again.

"Now," she murmured. "Please, Craig..."

"Not yet," he whispered back. "Not yet..."

"*Yes.*"

Her whisper was a demand, not a request, and he did smile then, a smile of loving softness in the darkness. His eyes, dark and intense, never left her face as his hands moved down in slow motion, teasing her taut, firm breasts, feeling the life surge through her body. His arousal brushed against her thighs, hot, aching. Her hands searched for him, and when he shifted slightly, she reached for his buttocks, trying to pull him to her.

He wanted to be inside her. He wanted to claim her flesh, her mind, her soul—to take her with such total possession that she would cry out for him. Her flesh was coated with damp silk; so was his. His hands were rough and then tender, fiercely possessive and then teasing.

He hadn't forgotten her nightmare. He couldn't. Guilt seared through him when he touched her; Sonia could not be more vulnerable than in loving, her limbs sprawled for him, uninhibited, Eve in desire, all woman in softness. He had risked her vulnerability another night, exactly that soft vulnerability...

"*Craig...*"

His palm glided down, over breasts and tummy and into the soft delta of hair between her thighs. Her limbs tightened, shuddering, when his finger slid into her warmth. His lips found hers in the darkness, found them and refused to let them go. His finger probed and withdrew, probed and withdrew.

Her whole body tightened, her breath rasping beneath his lips. He kissed that tremble of ecstasy, yet there was another and another and another before he let her sleep. She exploded for him; he could feel her burst free and keep on soaring. And when she finally leaned her head against him, exhausted, sleep claiming her, his lips brushed one last time against her forehead.

His own body throbbed with frustration, with exhaustion. It wasn't a choice, his own denial. His body refused him release, the weight of guilt for failing her like a wall too high, too thick, for him to escape.

"Charlie, do you know where Craig is?"

Charlie looked up from his steaming cup of coffee and morning paper. He looked a little startled at the broody brightness in Sonia's eyes, but his grin was natural. "He slipped out early." Charlie added wryly, "You look a little perkier than usual this morning; but then, I know better than to expect you to be cheerful in the morning. Coffee's on the stove."

Sonia smiled but didn't move from the doorway. "Did he say what time he'd be back?"

"Nope. Hopin' for midafternoon, but you know he'll get caught up until dinner."

"Yes." In jeans and bare feet and a crinkled red blouse, Sonia ambled forward to pour herself a cup of coffee. Every limb and muscle in her body vibrated this morning, but she felt edgy and unsure. She took a cautious sip of the hot brew, staring at the gray head turned away from her. Her eyes suddenly narrowed. "Charlie."

"Hmm."

Her voice was ultra quiet. "I think it's time you and I had a little talk."

Charlie's head whipped up again. "What's wrong?"

"Nothing. With me. It's Craig. And you know what's been bothering him, don't you?"

"What are you talking about? Nothing's bothering him."

But the knowledge was there in his eyes. Charlie was a terrible liar. Sonia perched on the chair next to him. "If I should happen to mention that I wanted to go into town this afternoon, what do you think my chances of going alone are? Will George miraculously need new parts from Brock's? And if I mention we're out of corn-flakes, are you going to suddenly rush into town so I won't go there *alone?*"

Charlie leaned back in his chair, snapped the newspaper, and promptly buried himself behind it. For several seconds, he said nothing, but in time he offered a grudging explanation. "No point in wasting gas when somebody on the ranch always needs something or other from a store."

"Hmm." Sonia took another sip of coffee. From around the newspaper, Charlie's weathered hand groped for his mug. The mug and hand disappeared again behind the pages of the business section. "I suppose if I ride out to my mother's, though," Sonia continued, "that would be perfectly all right."

"Nobody's ever stopped you from doing anything you want to do, and they never will, sprite. I don't know what you're talking about." Charlie crackled his paper again. "Now just drink your coffee until you're in a better mood."

"I'm in a better mood."

"Uh-uh. The whole place knows you're nasty until you've had your dose of caffeine. We all put up with you. You don't have to fake cheerfulness."

Charlie's teasing didn't fool her one bit. Sonia leaned forward and folded his newspaper down just a little. A definitely shifty pair of eyes only reluctantly met hers. "How long," she asked pleasantly, "has Craig been paying that man in Chicago, and exactly what is he supposed to be doing?"

Charlie's coffee splashed all over the paper. He lurched up from the table, fussing like a mother hen, grabbing a towel and flashing her a disgusted look.

"Answer me, Charlie." Sonia would have smiled at his antics ... any other time.

"I got stuff to do." He rapidly folded the paper and laid it on the table, set the cup on the counter, jammed his hat on.

Sonia said nothing.

Charlie tugged open the door and for an instant stood in the streaming morning sunlight. He turned, his wizened face in shadow. "Now, you just relax," he said uncomfortably. "You never did have a lick of patience first thing in the morning, and sometimes patience is just what's called for. So you just drink your coffee and let it all be, sprite. You hear me?"

Sonia took a second sip of coffee, studying him. Finally, she shook her head. "I don't think so."

"I've known that man longer than you have."

"Charlie—"

"Just bear with him awhile. Trust me, I know what I'm talking about." With a crisp little slam, he closed the door.

Sonia stared at the empty space for a moment, then picked up her coffee cup again. Charlie had always given her good advice.

But Charlie didn't have a husband who no longer wanted to make love. She'd woken up with a marvelous sense of well-being. Her body was sated, her hormones appeased; even her skin still tingled with the pleasure of having been loved and touched and ... taken care of. Fine.

Craig just didn't appear to need satisfaction for his own sake anymore. That was interesting. Miraculous, really.

Sonia's jaw firmed. She set down her empty cup. And felt totally lost inside.

An emerald in her belly button had not solved the problem. *What* problem? she asked herself, and slumped

back in the chair with her hands dug in her pockets.
Define the damn problem, Sonia.

Their lives, the ranch, and his work were fine. Her
man loved her; of that she had no doubt. If he wanted
to keep a few things from her temporarily, her inclination
was to trust him and ask no questions. In principle, privacy was just as important in a marriage as communication. If it weren't for their love life, Sonia would have
no reason at all to think that something was eating Craig
up alive.

Patience, Charlie had urged her. Which was a polite
way of saying, Shut up, Sonia. She'd never been very
good at shutting up. Not with Craig. Communication had
always been easy between them . . . but this, she had to
admit, was different. Coming out and asking a man why
he didn't want to make love to you—no. The other issues
were not very important. That one was. And that one,
she felt at the very frightened core of herself, was the
only issue that made a difference.

Craig pulled the Rover to a stop near the house, pock-
eted the key, and stepped out into the darkness. He immediately spotted the thin trail of white smoke meandering
up to the sky.

"Everything go all right today?" he questioned Charlie.

"Fine. Rounded up the strays in the north quarter."
Charlie lurched forward through the shadows, a cigar
clamped tight between his teeth. "You want to see the
new colt?"

"Is Sonia up?"

"She took it in her head to look over the half-year's
expenses," Charlie said delicately. "Been buried in the
study since dinner."

Craig chuckled, knowing that when Sonia insisted on
taking on the ranch bookkeeping, her concentration was
apt to affect her . . . amiability.

"You'll want to see the colt," Charlie said firmly.

Craig hesitated, a little amused at the faintly bellig-
erent note in Charlie's voice. All he really wanted to do
was pour himself a snifter of brandy and collapse on the
couch next to his wife after an exceedingly long day, but
for the moment he fell into step next to Charlie. "I'll go
to the stable for a minute or two," he agreed.

"Sure."

Charlie pushed open the doors. Stable smells assaulted
both of them, fresh hay and old leather and the scents
of the horses themselves. Charlie flicked a switch and
bright fluorescence promptly glowed on the central
walkthrough; a stallion at the far end whinnied his dis-
approval. Both men paused before the waist-high gates
of the nearest stall.

The colt was still wobbly, all legs and sleek brown
coat. Frightened eyes stared at them, ready to bolt. The
two men studied the animal. "Beautiful," Craig said softly.
"Oh, aren't you a beauty..."

The colt lifted his head, shaking it. Craig chuckled.
"They were fools to sell him," he said absently. "He's
magnificent. But he'll probably never get to stand at stud.
Sonia will take one look at him and turn him into a pet."

"You bought him for her."

"I wanted him for breeding stock."

"Bull." Charlie snorted.

Craig chuckled, and they both leaned over the rails
again, content to stare at the colt. Those wild eyes continued to stare at them; the colt tossed up his mane again.
Craig dug in his pocket and held out an open palm with
a sugar cube in it. The colt ignored it. Craig kept his
palm open, all patience.

"Sonia's on to you, you know," Charlie remarked with
studied idleness. "George never did have much subtlety."

Craig barely let on that he heard him, still wooing the
colt with his eyes.

"She heard me talking to Brenner in Chicago a few
nights ago."

The colt's eyes were on the sugar, his curiosity clearly

warring with his fear. The animal met Craig's eyes only
for an instant, and found there warmth and easy affection
and the promise of love and good care. His mane shivered
over his withers. Craig smiled, his palm steady.

Charlie shifted restlessly next to him. "I think," he
said mildly, "you'd both be better off if you could forget
the whole thing."

The colt ambled forward, close enough to get a whiff
of the sugar. And the man. He shied back with prancing
hooves, but Craig's hand never wavered. He kept his
voice as soft as butter so as not to scare the young animal.
"I'd almost talked myself into believing..." He hesitated. "And then she had a dream last night. Dreamed
the bastard was after her again." The colt dredged up a
new round of courage and edged forward again. "She
was shaking. Trembling so hard she couldn't stop.
Frightened. God knows how long she's been having
nightmares like that..."

The colt shied away from him, eyes wide, ears back,
as if he sensed the tension in the man. Still, he probed
the palm until he found the sugar. Once he had claimed
it, he bolted to the back of the stall again. Craig turned,
staring at Charlie.

His voice changed just that quickly. The tone held
nothing that would have raised fear in the colt, but the
iron firmness was unmistakable. "You didn't know me
when my father died, and you never saw me in my first
brawl. We've known each other a long time, though,
Charlie. You saw me the day I got back from the bank,
when they said I couldn't save this damn ranch. You
remember that Raker fool who thought he could buy the
place out from under me? He thought he could buy the
place out from under me? He thought I was a greenhorn
nineteen-year-old kid. And I was. Stupid and arrogant
and with far more guts than brains, but I always fought
my own battles."

"Now, look—" Charlie started in a low voice.

"I've fought for every damn thing I've ever had. You

think I couldn't protect her?" Craig demanded. "I'd kill anyone who harmed her," he said softly. "And I'd do it without blinking an eye. The decision would be simple. Because if anyone touched her—"

"Hey," Charlie said uncomfortably.

"There's no point in telling me to forget about it, Charlie. I hear what you're trying to say, and to some extent you're right. I can't pen her in. That wouldn't work. But I mean to see to it that *nothing* like that ever happens to her again. You hear me?"

Charlie hesitated. He drew the cigar from his mouth, and his eyes dropped from Craig's steadfast stare. "I hear you," he said flatly.

"Good." Craig walked over and switched off the light, holding the stable door open for both of them. He said nothing else until Charlie headed toward his own house, and then called out mildly, "That's the first time I've seen you smoke in the stable in years. You still upset now?"

Charlie didn't answer.

"Because if you want to keep arguing, Charlie, we'll argue. Just tell me how you'd feel if it were your own woman."

Charlie didn't even turn around. "'Bout time we both got some shut-eye." He chomped on the cigar again.

They both headed toward home.

10

"YOU *SURE* YOU know what you're doing?" Charlie said.

"I'm sure I know what I'm doing," Sonia affirmed.

"It's not like it would be any bother for me to wait a few minutes for you." Charlie sent her a sidelong glance as he slammed his boot on the brake in the parking lot. "He's been working every night this week."

"Believe me, I know that."

"And if he's smack dab in the middle of something, you're going to be stuck waiting around."

"I will not be stuck," Sonia promised firmly.

"I just can't see stranding you..."

Leaning across the pickup seat, she pressed a very firm, very affectionate smack on Charlie's cheek. "I refuse to say it another time. Now just get out of here and stop feeling guilty, would you, Charlie? If worse comes to worst, I can drive Craig's car home and then come back and pick him up later."

Charlie shot her a disapproving glance. She escaped from the pickup before he could argue any further, and waved at him cheerfully until he had no choice but to back up and zoom away.

Alone, she took a massive breath into her lungs and stood in front of Craig's office, feeling miserably stranded.

A late afternoon wind whipped her skirts up to her thighs and cavorted with her once-perfect hairstyle. Wind or no, the temperature had to be climbing past ninety.

The predatory sun spotted its lone victim and attacked, baking her instantly from her crown to her toes. Still, Sonia stood motionless for a minute, and then turned restlessly, staring at the office door as she wandered toward it.

She'd pushed that door open dozens of times, but never dressed in gold earrings and gold belt and gold sandals. The only other thing she wore was a very simple little white silk jersey dress with a flowing skirt and draped bodice and a few crisscross straps in back. White was a symbol of virtue, though the dress lacked something along those lines. The soft material draped and flowed around her figure in a way that suggested a great many things, and none of them virtuous. Furthermore, she hadn't a stitch on underneath it.

There was no question that it took more nerve than brains to show up at the office in such attire.

She was dressed for seduction, which was rather ironic, since sex was absolutely the last thing on her mind. Diverting her husband was on her mind. Women who played sexual games to get what they wanted had always disgusted her. On the other hand, when one was desperate, one used the weapons at hand.

She hadn't known what else to do. Her world wasn't exactly crumbling—just tipping precariously. Craig had been avoiding her this past week. His excuse was twelve-hour work days; her instincts told her otherwise. And in those same twelve-hour days, Sonia had shamelessly plotted to get her husband alone. A vacation for just the two of them was her goal...but if Craig wouldn't go? If he really didn't want to be alone with her...

Fear was a funny thing. She'd felt fear in Chicago. This was a different fear, far more threatening. She felt as if she were fighting a ghost she couldn't see face to face. As if there were a mountain between her and Craig and she didn't know how to cross it.

She had to try.

Renewed determination bolstered her flagging confidence, and she firmly pushed open the door. Cool air and silence greated her, both reasonably calming the flutter of nerves in her head. Stubbornness sparkled in her eyes as she neared the sound of Mrs. Heath's type-writer outside Craig's office.

The older woman glanced up, her surprised smile as quick as the welcome in her dark gray eyes. "Mrs. Hamilton! I certainly didn't expect to see you here!"

"I know, Mrs. Heath, and Craig doesn't expect me either." She hesitated. "Am I going to be in terrible hot water if I steal him away to dinner?" she whispered.

The other woman chuckled, her eyes whisking over Sonia's attire approvingly. "Trouble?" she whispered back. "You'll get a medal from all of us. Get that man out of our hair for a while! He's been driving us all nuts this past week. Crises are one thing, but even in the best of times I swear that man never takes a coffee break."

Sonia nodded. "I had a feeling he was overdoing it." She motioned toward the closed door. "Anyone with him?"

"Just John. I can—"

"It's all right. I'll wait."

They chatted a few minutes more; it wasn't long before the inner office door opened. Sonia saw John's back first. He kept his hand on the doorknob as he continued talking pressure tolerances and other technical problems. Then he glanced around and spotted Sonia. His long, low wolf whistle immediately terminated that conversation.

Craig's head immediately whipped around the door, annoyance radiating from him even before he'd recognized the source of irritation. The source promptly vaulted in his general direction. "Hi," she said simply, offering a secret wink for Mrs. Heath, and seconds later closed the door on John, Mrs. Heath, and the rest of the world.

For at least an instant, she had one stunned husband on her hands. One had to take all the breaks one was offered in life. She stole a quick glance, only long enough to see what she already knew. Craig's shirtsleeves were rolled up, there were hollows under his eyes, his hair looked as if his hands had run through it a dozen times that day, and his tie was askew. He looked, quite simply, exhausted. A man determined to drive himself too hard and too long.

"We're going out to dinner," she announced blithely. "I don't want to hear any arguments. We're going to drink a little wine, eat a very expensive steak..."

"Sonia? When on earth did you get here? How—?"

"At the Red Baron. We haven't been there in ages. And if I were you, I wouldn't put my hand anywhere near that briefcase, because you are definitely not taking it home tonight." She spotted his suit jacket on the chair where he'd undoubtedly thrown it that morning. She moved to pick it up, then changed her mind. "This jacket is too hot," she continued in the same brisk tone, "but we have to do a little something about your appearance before we go. Not much," she assured him, with slightly more gentleness.

Her pulse was frantic as she approached him with quick steps, staring at his throat as she rebuttoned the collar of his shirt. His body was warm against her palm. Warm and still and tense. She tugged at his tie.

"I don't want to hear any excuses," she said severely. "If the whole place falls apart because you're gone for a couple of hours, then it's just going to have to fall apart. Mrs. Heath can order everyone around while you're gone. She's already agreed." Sonia was having a terrible time with the tie, primarily because her fingers were all thumbs. She darted a quick glance up, to see how Craig was taking all the bossing.

She relaxed, her fingers suddenly managing the tie just fine. His weary eyes had a slight hint of exasperation, but his upper lip was twitching. "I get the idea I'm supposed to feel kidnapped," he said mildly.

She stood back, hands on hips, pretending to make sure the tie was straight, knowing she couldn't care less about the tie. "You'll be lucky if you get off with a kidnapping," she informed him.

"Now I'm really shaking in my shoes."

She chuckled. Godzilla couldn't make that man shake in his shoes, and Craig was just getting around to noticing her dress. Actually, he seemed to be noticing everything but the dress. She could feel the warmth of his gaze on her bare legs and bare throat and bare back as if it were the heat of the sun. Hurriedly, she picked up his jacket. "I'll carry this."

"Would you mind," he asked gravely, "if I make a single phone call first?"

She shook her head. "Absolutely no phone calls. Any good kidnapping has to be pulled off clean. Give an inch and next thing you know the victim will be asking for ransom."

"You sound quite experienced."

"I started young in a life of crime." She hesitated at the door, her tone abruptly, softly, Sonia again. "Craig, for heaven's sake, if you really need to make a phone call—"

He made a swift motion toward the phone and then stopped, turning back to her. "It'll wait," he said gravely. "There's no way I'm going to be late for my own kidnapping." He opened the door.

The Red Baron was Cold Creek's long-established hideaway for a nice seductive dinner. Candles set in red glass decorated every table; dark paneled walls and thick carpeting and tasteful oils on the walls added to a serenely luxurious atmosphere. A pocket-sized dance floor in the far corner included a pianist and bass player; the music was muted and low.

Craig glanced up as the busboy took their plates. When the man had gone, Craig watched Sonia lean over and tip a little more wine into his glass. That was his third, and she had barely touched her first.

At the moment, he was bone weary, sated from an

absolutely delicious dinner, and utterly intrigued by the lady across from him. Sooner or later, he would figure out what she was up to.

The clues to the mystery were most interesting. The look of her would have seduced a monk, she'd chosen the most romantic place in town, and she'd been plying him with wine. Furthermore, she'd set out to relax him over dinner as if it were her life's purpose. The talk had all been simple and easy, her low, sweet laughter wafting toward him at intervals, her teasing sassy. He could smell her perfume; when she leaned toward him her bodice flirted with his eyes; and as she talked, those eyelashes of hers floated up and down with all the skill of a practiced flirt.

All those clues seemed conclusive. He hadn't been fooled by her act from the time she'd excused herself for a second trip to the ladies' room. Sonia was nervous. Those fluttering eyelashes shielded eyes that remarkably kept missing direct contact. All that subtly offered sexuality was a blind.

A blind that was working with aching intensity inside his bloodstream. He'd been aroused from the minute they sat down, and he hadn't even touched her. She had shied away from his touch; her game was all in look and scent and the low, soothing melody of her voice.

Deprivation was doing strange things to his rational thinking processes. He wanted his wife. He also knew that the moment he tried to make love to her again, that living nightmare of his would be back. He'd tried working endless hours; he'd tried avoiding her; and he'd tried giving himself time. Nothing had worked. Guilt seeped into him like an insidious poison. There wasn't even a ghost of a chance of allowing himself his own sexual release.

Only that same physical deprivation was starting to add up to a little mountain of agony. It was almost funny. His hormones hadn't been this active when he was a teenager.

He listened to her laugh at something he said, a sparkle of wine glistening on her bottom lip, her aquamarine eyes glowing like melted jewels, and wondered vaguely what she would do if he took her outside, leaned her up against a building, slipped those smooth, silky skirts up . . .

"Do you want more coffee?" he asked calmly as the waiter hovered over them.

She shook her head.

He watched her eyes dart to the dance floor for the third time. She wouldn't ask; she knew he was tired. Good. There was no way on earth he wanted to risk touching her at all. No sane man invited torture.

"Craig?" She parted her lips to say something. It was the third time she'd done that, yet again she seemed to change her mind about what she wanted to say. "Darn it. I suppose we should be going home," she remarked lightly.

"Not quite yet." He set his napkin down and stood up. "Not yet," he murmured again. A pulse flickered dangerously in his neck as he motioned her toward the dance floor. Her delighted smile made something in his jaw tighten. His palm lightly brushed the small of her back as he guided her around tables, so lightly that his fingertips only barely burned from the contact of the cool, silky fabric of her dress.

He meant to keep her at arm's length when they were on the dance floor. The song was a love song, but not a favorite, unfamiliar, nothing that stirred any nostalgic, suggestive longings. He turned her to him and raised his hand simply to take hers . . . and instead found that damned errant hand sliding up her bare arm to her neck. And then the other one, just as damned, gliding around to the bare flesh of her back.

Sonia started and then ever so naturally moved in to him, her arms wrapping loosely around his waist, her cheek tucked into the curve of his shoulder. She made a small contented sound like the purr of a kitten as they moved in a gentle sway around the dance floor.

The first song ended, and another started. From no-where, she suddenly lifted her head, her hooded blue-green eyes studying him. "Craig?"

"Hmm?"

"Nothing." Her eyelashes rushed back down. "This feels good. We haven't danced in forever."

His lips pressed lightly on her forehead. "I think you'd better get around to telling me," he whispered.

"Telling you what?"

"Whatever it is that's been bothering you."

She lifted her head again, her eyes suddenly flashing with amused exasperation. She hated it when he out-thought her. "Nothing's bothering me."

His hands slid down her back in a slow caress, taking in her warm, smooth skin beneath the silky straps of her dress, taking in the shape of her spine and that narrow tapering at her waist. His voice was seductively gentle. "You wrecked the car."

"Of course not!" Her head whipped back again, this time most indignantly.

His lips found the tip of her nose. "You gave the state trooper a merry chase on the highway again."

"I haven't had a ticket in over two years," she re-minded him.

"That you confessed to."

"That I—there was only one other one," she said irritably. "How did you—"

"So it isn't that. You've overcharged on every account we have, and we're both going to the poorhouse?"

She couldn't help chuckling at his off-the-wall guesses. The pianist switched tunes, and she nuzzled her face close to Craig's cheek, her arms moving up and around him where her fingers could reach the curling hair at the nape of his neck.

"Sonia..." he warned teasingly.

"Yes." She sighed. "The thing is, what do you think about the Gulf of Mexico?"

"Pardon?"

"The Gulf of Mexico."

"I think it's a very nice body of water," he said blandly, but when he tried to tilt his head to take a curious look at her, her cheek stayed molded to his shoulder.

"I like it, too," she remarked.

"That's nice."

"What do you think about boats?"

"Does this conversation strike you as a little unusual, or is it me?"

"I like boats, myself," Sonia continued stubbornly.

"I like boats, too. I suppose. Both of us having lived most of our lives in Wyoming, boats have just never been given a high priority."

"You've been fishing with my dad up in the mountains," she reminded him quickly. "You liked that boat."

"Yes," Craig agreed wryly. "I'm extremely fond of rowboats."

"And big boats aren't very different from little boats. They both float, for instance. Actually, big boats can be very easy to run."

"Is that so?"

"That's so." Sonia took a huge breath. "I've found one that's very easy to run. In the Gulf of Mexico. For four days. Starting Sunday." One of them suddenly wasn't dancing, but Sonia stayed firmly entrenched within the relative safety of his arms until he recovered a little from the shock. "I had to think of something to give you for our anniversary..."

"Our anniversary is six months away."

"I've never remembered dates well," she reminded him.

"Sonia," he growled impatiently into her temple.

"It's called a tri-cabin cruiser. A baby could run it, the man said. Everything's taken care of—transportation, tickets, insurance. I talked to Mrs. Heath; she said next week wouldn't be a bad time for you to leave. Charlie, by the grace of God, doesn't mind taking care of things—"

"You've had one hell of a busy week," he said abruptly.

"A little," she agreed demurely. She'd only stopped panting that afternoon.

Her husband was silent for a time. The second love song stretched to a third one, a ballad about love and loss and tender memories. About the time of the second refrain, some of the stiffness seemed most unwillingly to rush from his body; he gathered her close again. His fingertips glided up and down, up and down, over her back in the rhythm of caress, the rhythm of intimacy.

She could feel the sway of her skirts against him and the softness of her breasts against his chest . . . and the arousal he was no longer trying to hide from her. Even massive shocks, she noted, had not appreciably affected the size or heat of that arousal. Through two layers of clothes, she could clearly feel him.

One of his hands strayed down to her hips, and lingered. She waited. His hand slipped back up to more appropriate territory, but after a time she heard the breath hiss from his lungs.

"You're not wearing a damn thing under that dress," he whispered in her ear.

"No," she admitted. Dancing eyes suddenly peered up at him. "It was part of the campaign to distract you, so you would say yes," she commented demurely. "Are you distracted?"

"Have you considered what it would look like if I dragged you down in the middle of this dance floor?"

Lord, he was suddenly restless. His voice was a low-pitched growl in her ear. He was moving to the rhythm of some song that certainly wasn't what the pianist was playing. Craig's song was infinitely slower, one about possession and fierce, swift loving. Sonia didn't know the words, but she knew well the music of his body and understood in every feminine bone in her body the tempo his heartbeat was picking up.

"Are we going?" she whispered finally.

She studied the play of emotions on his face with an anxious feeling of waiting inside. He didn't want to go;

she knew that. He was looking for a way to say no to her. She could almost see him cataloging the problems in his head, from his work to the ranch, from timing to expense. Those, she knew, could be worked out.

She also knew he had never refused her anything that she had really wanted. And that, in the end, was what would make the difference, weigh in the balance against whatever reasons he really had for not wanting to be alone with her.

Her fingertips grazed his jawline, her soft eyes searching his, the frivolity gone. "It's all right either way, Craig," she said softly. "I just . . . love you. All I wanted was some special time with you, but if we absolutely can't . . ."

There was so much tension in his face, a jagged, taut anxiety set in proud lines. And in the layer under that, she could not mistake the searing depth of sheer, rich love in his eyes. "So," he said quietly, "what time did you say the plane leaves on Sunday?"

Craig jerked the pillow behind him and leaned up against it, tossing his trade magazine on the floor. Sonia was in the bathroom. He could hear her brushing her teeth.

He'd come home fully expecting Sonia to strip to the buff from her wanton white dress. She had, but out of sight in the bathroom. She'd appeared moments later in some granny nightgown he'd never seen before, and disappeared again. The next time her head darted around the door, there were gobs of white cream all over her face. Once he'd gotten a good look at that, she'd vanished again.

She'd been chattering about the trip to the Gulf the entire time, but the message that his lady had withdrawn from her irresistible-wench mood was unmistakable. She'd never before put white gunk on her face, and that blasted nightgown had come out of some attic.

In one sense he was amused, and perhaps even relieved she was...out of the mood. In another sense, he felt more restless than a hungry cougar on the prowl. His own problems were not Sonia's, and he'd had every intention of taking up her sexual challenge. He did *not* understand her mercurial mood. Her taking off the dress in the bathroom amounted to cruel and unusual punishment, and his own head seemed to be in so many confused places at once that, disgusted, he picked up the magazine yet a third time.

Sonia, yawning, stepped out of the bathroom, this time flicking off the light, her hair brushed and her face clean and soft under the lamplight: "Must have been that wine at dinner, but I am unbelievably sleepy. You must be, too, after all the hours you've put in this week."

"A little," he agreed.

She slipped between the sheets next to him. He immediately turned off the light, tossed aside the magazine, and slid down next to her. Automatically, he tucked the sheet around her chin and then, beneath the covers, reached across her side, her signal to turn over and move in closer, the way she always liked to sleep.

She didn't move.

He didn't really pay much attention. A silent yawn rumbled from his lips; the week's exhaustion was taking its toll. Instinctively, his arm slid around her again, but instead of rolling over, she flopped on her stomach, her face turned to the far wall. He stiffened. Sonia never broke her sleep patterns; he couldn't remember a time when they hadn't fallen asleep in the same way. For himself, he could crash anywhere and anytime. It was his wife who couldn't fall asleep unless she was tucked and curled and cuddled exactly just so.

He listened, hearing the sound of her even breathing, Carefully, silently, and a little stubbornly, he shifted both of them. Her body was limp; she murmured something but didn't stir. It took a few moments, because he really didn't want to wake her, but in time he had it right again. Her leg was tucked between his, her cheek in his shoulder, his arm protectively curled around her, resting on her thigh. Finally, his eyes closed.

Sonia's opened, facing the wall of his chest, her body as supple as grass in the wind, her mind racing at full speed. Her husband was finally asleep. He didn't know what was going on yet, but he would.

We have a marriage here, Mr. Hamilton, which means sacrifices are occasionally required, she told him silently. That goes for both of us. Because if you're giving up sex, buster, then so am I.

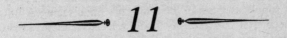

11

MR. BARTHOLOMEW GRINNED at them from the dock. "Have a wonderful time, you two! Any problems, you just give me a little ship-to-shore," he called over the rising roar of the engine.

He motioned to Sonia and, laughing, she leaned over the side, expecting the precarious buss on the cheek that she got. "Don't you worry about that husband of yours, honey," the marina owner told her. "He knows more about boats than probably half the people on the Gulf. You just get yourself a solid honeymoon going there." He winked lasciviously before ambling his portly body to the dock edge, where he untied the first line and tossed it to her.

She was still coiling the last line as Craig slowly maneuvered the cruiser out of the crowded marina and into open waters. Waving one final time at the distant form of Mr. Bartholomew, Sonia turned toward the sun, and then exuberantly bolted up the five steps to Craig at the wheel.

He didn't much look like a yacht owner, dressed in cutoffs and sneakers. Sonia perched on the matching captain's chair next to him, tossing him a happy grin as she slipped her sunglasses down from the top of her head and onto her nose again. From behind that cover she was free to feast on his sun-browned skin and half-naked torso . . . in between checking out a sky that looked burned-on blue, a grape-winged gull soaring overhead, and the endless waters of the Gulf foaming behind them.

"What'd that dirty old man say to you?" Craig demanded.

She chuckled. "That you had more experience on the water than half the people who rent boats around here."

"That man talks more drivel than a stand-up comedian." The shore waters by the marina were peppered with sailboats and weekend cruisers. Craig risked only a single glance at his wife.

She could feel the assessment in his eyes as he took in her nautical white short shorts and T-shirt with anchors. The anchors were strategically placed, to rise and fall with every breath. "You know . . ." She tried to make her voice mild, which wasn't that easy over the roar of the engines. "I thought I had everything so perfectly arranged that you wouldn't have to do a thing. The plane tickets, transportation to the marina, food ordered ahead, insurance, the boat rental . . ."

"You did." Craig spared her another quick glance.

"But somehow it never occurred to me that there was a little more involved. Licensing, navigation laws, setting courses, docking facilities." It hadn't occurred to her because all she'd had in mind was leaving a dock, throwing out an anchor in the middle of the Gulf somewhere, and having her husband alone at her mercy for four days. She did not, for the moment, mention that. "Engine rooms, fuel tanks, electrical backups," she droned on. "Amazing how fast you picked it all up."

Craig shot her an unholy grin. "I listened to Bartholomew for three hours last night."

"Bull," Sonia said sweetly. "Who was she?"

"Pardon?"

"I said, Mr. Hamilton-of-landlocked-Wyoming, *who was she?*"

"Who was who?"

"You didn't come by all that boat expertise honestly, buster. Now, I always like to think of them as poor substitutes. *Not* rich yacht owners."

"Who?" Craig's brow flexed in a quizzical frown.

"Your former girl friends." Sonia slid off the leather seat, peering at him severely over the rims of her sunglasses, and announced, "I'm going below to get a soda. For me. You're in hot water. So you're a big fan of rowboats, are you? Isn't that what you told me at dinner the other night?"

His arm snaked around her ribs before she could take the first step down. Even as his hand again touched the wheel and stayed firmly there, he managed to haul her tight to his chest and take a quick teasing nip out of her neck before he released her again. "I've told you a thousand times, I was a virgin when I met you," he reminded her.

"Send that one to Ripley's," Sonia said flatly. "Not once—not *once*—have you ever told me one good sordid story about your past lovers."

"Because I didn't have any."

Sonia sighed. "The very *least* you could do is tell me she was ugly," she insisted.

"Who?"

"The girl who taught you more than you needed to know about boats."

"She was ugly," Craig obliged.

"Pockmarked."

"Pockmarked," he agreed gravely.

"Buck teeth."

"No orthodontist could have helped her."

"Dull."

"Dull," he said, choking with laughter.

"And it was definitely a platonic relationship."

"You bet."

"All right," Sonia said grudgingly. "You've earned your soda. Only because I *know* you would never lie to me." She headed for the steps.

"Sonia," he called after her. "They *were* all poor substitutes."

Chuckling, she climbed down to the salon, and paused for a moment in sheer appreciation. The powder-blue

couch and chairs had navy piping and pillows, a color
scheme accented by hand-rubbed teak bulkheads. The
furniture fabric was velvet, dreadfully impractical and
delightfully luxurious. Her sneakers bounced on the
spongy carpet, *definitely* a carpet that called for bare feet.
The cruiser was everything she'd been promised on the
phone, and more.

The forward cabin was set up like a study, with couches
and bookshelves. Toward the back of the boat—aft, she
reminded herself for the ninth time—was their master
stateroom. Centered therein was a queen-sized bed. The
pillows were down-filled, the sheets were satin, and the
comforter was a cloud-soft pale blue. Diverted from her
search for cold drinks, Sonia leaned thoughtfully in the
doorway, staring at that bed.

She had rather dangerous plans for that bed. Dangerous because there was no guarantee they would work.
There didn't seem to be any convenient rule books on
how to turn one very unselfish lover into a selfish one.
The only thing Sonia was absolutely sure of was that
there would be no more one-sided satisfaction. One very
stubborn, enigmatic, extremely well-loved man was about
to get his due, or there would be no more encounters of
any kind, on that bed or any other.

Her game plan was very simple. All she had in mind
was giving her husband an intensive course in total sexual
frustration.

*And if that doesn't work? Darn it, if he really doesn't
want to make love with you* ... Taking another glance
at the bed and plump, stuffed pillows, she sighed worriedly, lifted her chin, and headed back through the salon.

A teak railing and three steps up separated the kitchen
from the main salon. Sonia removed two cans of cola
from the refrigerator and then randomly opened cup-
boards and drawers. The diminutive galley delighted her,
from the microwave to the grill to the itsy-bitsy dishwasher. More important, it was stocked with every goodie
Craig had ever expressed a liking for, from steak and

baby crab to cooling bottles of Orvieto and Cabernet Sauvignon.

Everything was there. Snatching up the Cokes, she raced pell-mell up to Craig again.

He'd missed her, he thought fleetingly, in those short ten minutes. Exactly how long had it been since he'd been totally alone with his wife for a few stolen days? And a most puzzling mood had been stealing up on him from the moment they'd arrived near the Gulf Coast of Texas. A contrary, inexplicable mood.

It had something to do with endless sun and ocean smells and lazy, lazy winds. Relaxation had slowly been creeping up on him like a drug; he'd almost forgotten what it was like to feel . . . easy. Not just with Sonia, but with himself.

His right to touch his wife, his sense of failure about himself as a man . . . these feelings hadn't disappeared, but for the moment seemed involuntarily shifted into another part of his being. Increasingly, all Sonia had to do was slip out of sight and he was impatient for her to come back. He craved, desired, wanted, needed her, and he was becoming rather obsessed by the wanton urge to take Sonia, to love her, to make love to her, to feel her sheathed softness around him.

His soul was beginning to feel as if it had been spun in a blender.

It didn't help when Sonia bolted up the steps with the cans of cola in her hands, laughing as if just the breeze alone delighted her, the sun dancing in her hair and her limbs blithely displayed in front of him as she leaned against the opposite chair.

"I'll open your soda for you," she told him cheerfully, and popped the top, chuckling as the cola foamed. Her tongue swooped down and lapped at the burgeoning foam before she handed it to him. "That'll teach me to run up the stairs carrying carbonated pop, don't you think?" she asked dryly.

He didn't know. He was too busy following the path of her tongue, the faint moisture on her lips, as he accepted the can. He took a long gulp, though his thirst was not for any carbonated drink. "Thanks," he murmured, just a slight edge of irony in his tone.

"I'm broiling." Taking the hem of her top in her fingers, she lifted it up, tugged it over her head, and pulled it off. Seconds later she had skimmed her white terrycloth shorts down to her ankles and bent over to step out of them. "Better," she announced.

Better? he thought roughly. *Better?* Her bikini was scarlet. A set of three bows and some string. The expanse of Sonia's white skin was exactly the measure of what skin had never been touched directly by the sun before, no matter how often she swam in her mother's pool.

"New suit?" he said flatly.

"Hmm." Sonia took a sip of her drink and despaired. The suit *should have* brought some reaction. Heaven knew, if a sea gull had winged close, she would have blushed.

She took a second sip of pop, again set the can down, and regarded her husband from behind her dark lenses with a determined expression. "Are you going to show me how to pilot this thing, Captain?" she asked lightly.

Before he'd had the chance to say a word, she slipped down from her stool, ducked under his arm, and angled in front of him. A panoply of shining dials confronted her. Behind her were Craig's cutoffs and muscular brown legs. She leaned lazily backward until her hips were cradled in his spread thighs. "Where," she questioned, "is the throttle?"

Craig didn't answer for a moment. When he did, his voice was thick and low. "Sonia—" His throat appeared to unclog. "There are two. Here. You have to move them both at the same time."

"No problem," she informed him. Her fingers experimented with the little levers. Within seconds, the steady slice of the prow turned into a chop, chop, chop, as the boat burrowed through the waters, spitting out an incredible wake of bubbling white froth behind them. "How long before we get to the little cove Mr. Bartholomew told us about?"

Craig's voice was totally controlled, and rather dry. "About a minute and a half, assuming we maintain this death-defying speed. About two hours, otherwise."

Sonia's head tilted back, her hair curling on his bare shoulders as he glanced down at her upturned grin. "Was that a subtle suggestion that I slow down?" she asked.

"That rather depends on whether or not you value life." He did. Hers. The look and feel of her windswept hair and her impudent red lips parted in laughter... Strands of hair were lacing across her forehead, her cheeks. He lifted his hand, intending to smooth them back.

Sonia saw his arm rise, just as she saw that instant's hesitation before his hand touched her. She'd been waiting for him to make that move. "You win," she announced cheerfully, and swiftly, smoothly, slid under his other arm and away. "Obviously, my driving skills are totally unappreciated here. You will find me," she informed him, "on the upper deck. Having a love affair with the sun."

Her sea legs were still a little precarious, but she held on to the rail as she wandered up to the top deck of the boat. Water splashed up, sprinkling her with an ice-cold spray in direct contrast to the steadily baking sun, making her laugh. Above, the white deck was hot, but not unbearably so.

Slipping off her sneakers, she stretched out on her back, wishing she'd brought a towel and deciding that for the immediate present she could do without one. The day stretched in front of her with endless possibilities; and if her mind had been churning out anxieties and plans at miles per minute, her body paused simply to take in all the luxuries of sun and water, all the new smells and new sounds.

After a time, she turned over on her stomach, lifted her head, and smiled at Craig. A sun visor separated them, along with perhaps three feet of distance, and Craig was standing at the helm; she could only see his face when she raised her head up so high. She gave him a lazy wave and lowered her head again. After a moment, she glanced on both sides of the boat, saw absolutely no other sail or vessel at all, and reached back to untie her bikini top.

In seconds, the wispy garment sailed over the visor. She lifted her head up just for an instant, to make sure that Craig had caught it.

He had. The skinny band of material was clenched in his fist. There was a nice little pulse hammering at the base of his throat.

Smiling, she cradled her head on her arms and closed her eyes.

They had anchored in a half-moon cove that looked for all the world like the tiny harbor of their own private deserted island. Sunset colors shimmered through the still palms, and the sandy beach in the distance had the glow of gold. Gulls soared overhead as if they had nothing better to do than glide free in those last moments of day.

The water slip-slopped against the boat's hull in an endless, rhythmic sway that was half lullaby, half sensual call to the senses. A hush had fallen with evening. The wind had died, and the heat had become something alive and lazy and hypnotically soothing. Craig leaned over the rails, watching the silver fin of a fish just beneath the water. Behind him, the grill continued to glow with dying coals. Dinner was over, and he absently drank the last of his wine.

"Craig!"

He turned quickly and strode to the steps in time to catch the falling bundle in Sonia's arms. "What on earth are you—"

"Guess what! I found a telescope below," she explained, laughing as she set down the rest of her armload.

Craig noted her other choices with amusement. One blanket, two pillows, one bowl of grapes, two clean glasses, one additional bottle of wine when they weren't even close to finishing the first one yet, and yes, a sort of portable telescope. "We needed the grapes to look at the stars?" he questioned wryly.

She stuffed one into his mouth. "Not *specifically,* but generally, yes," she chided him. "Every normal human being suffers constant hunger pangs when spending a day on the water. Look how much we ate for dinner."

"We?" Craig teased.

"Waste not, want not." Sonia glowered darkly.

"Is *that* why you raced through nearly two steaks all on your own?"

She nodded impishly. "And you're going to pay for this trip when we get home with a week of cottage cheese, if you can't control my appetite better than that, Mr. Hamilton." She turned away, to bend over and spread out the blanket on the deck.

"In that case, perhaps I'd better take control over all of your appetites, Mrs. Hamilton."

Her fingers stilled on the blanket, and then she gave it a vigorous shake. Amazing, how quickly sensuous images could dance through her bloodstream.

She hadn't kissed her husband in twenty-four hours now. Fourteen hundred and forty minutes. Withdrawal pangs had set in about fourteen hundred minutes ago. To the devil with sex. Affection, just *touching,* had always been part of their relationship. And her heart was regularly beating out a reminder that plans or no plans, a man in trouble needed all the affection and compassion she could give him.

Still, love and attention she had given freely. It hadn't erased the haunted look in her husband's eyes. Other action, drastic action, had been called for.

Fine. Well, actually that wasn't fine at all, because keeping him at a good distance meant not only that he couldn't touch her, but that she couldn't touch him either.

Craig swiftly moved beside her, fixing the blanket she couldn't seem to smooth out to save her life. He cast her a quick smile, one of his most lethal playful ones. He'd changed into canvas shorts for dinner; she'd dressed just as informally in a black maillot bathing suit with sexy holes up and down the sides. For the instant, though, she couldn't seem to get into the role of tease. All she wanted to do was grab those sun-browned shoulders and hold that huge man so tight, so hard, so...

"Cat got your tongue?" he teased. "All this silence is so rare I can barely stand it."

"You," she said disgustedly, but the feeling wouldn't leave her so easily. He needed some good, solid loving, that man. He'd been easy and tender and *special* all day, which made yet another ball of anxiety tighten inside her. What exactly was it going to take to get him to loosen up and admit what was bothering him? It hurt, that he believed he was fooling her. "Now," she said, all businesslike as she plumped the pillows, "we have one night, one sky full of stars, and one telescope. For once in my life, I'd like to locate more than the Big Dipper."

He slid down beside her with a chuckle. "I wasn't aware of this terrible gap in your education."

"I don't admit it to everyone." Lying on the deck, she reached over him for the wine, and poured him a glass. "We have to do something until it gets dark enough. I figured I'd play Roman slave girl to your Nero. You lie there, and I'll feed you grapes and wine."

Blue eyes rested on hers. A lightning storm crackled from nowhere. The sky was cloudless and there wasn't the hint of a breeze, but somewhere between his eyes and hers there was searing tension, a crackling aware-ness... "You do like that idea, don't you?" Her voice was oddly low, working to keep the teasing tone in it. "The lady at your mercy, to do with what you will?"

"I like the idea." His palm brushed in her hair, smoothing it back. "Not of Nero, not of slave girls. But of you feeding me grapes and wine, on a boat with no one around, on a night when no one can hear us. Do you know what I'd like to do to you?"

His eyes gave her a very good idea. She searched his face. Darkness had fallen so rapidly that his eyes had a luminous quality, all the intensity of luster, all the softness of the dark waters surrounding them. He wanted to touch her; he wanted to love her; she could feel it clear to her soul. Her spine tingled with it.

But would it be the same, would he make love *to* her but not *with* her, would he give only for her pleasure?

His eyes made lush, erotic promises to her . . . yet his body spoke of control. Control where he was concerned.

Leaning her cheek to his palm, she pressed her lips there softly and then withdrew. She picked up a grape and raised the sweet fruit to his lips. "Enjoy, Nero," she commanded brightly. "Your time will come. First, the stars."

She could feel him staring at her as she busied herself with the telescope, handing him his wine again, chattering. Naturally, he was staring; she'd never behaved like such a fool in her life! Still, he let her play out her games without a word, and in time she relaxed.

Twenty minutes later, stretched flat, she had the telescope to her eye and was squinting into it as she swung it back and forth across the sky. "This is hopeless," she complained. "I can't even find the North Star."

Craig tugged the telescope from her hands and pointed it at the brightest diamond above. One could hardly miss it.

She gave him a severe look for the chuckle he was barely holding back. "I *know* it's up there. But it disappears when you put the lens to your eye."

He sighed. "How can one extremely intelligent woman be such an occasional dunce?" he questioned the heavens.

"Oh, hush." She put the telescope back in its box, stood up, and stretched. "I knew all along I should have married Mack McPherson. Never, *never*, would he have made fun of me."

His eyes trailed the length of her long, sleek legs in the moonlight. *"Who* is Mack McPherson?"

"Didn't I ever mention him? You dragged everything else out of me. Without once," she added plaintively, "revealing one interesting detail about your own past love life."

"Mack," he reminded her.

"Mack was the high school heartthrob." she said with a grin. "The Mr. Cool of Cold Creek High. Basketball star, big man in school politics, the local tycoon's son—and also my first date." Sonia's lashes lowered as she took a thoughtful look at her husband. He wasn't scowling, because Craig was far too mature to give in to anything as childish as jealousy. He just looked...irritated. Definitely irritated.

While she had his attention, she slowly stood up, and receded just slightly into the shadows. When Craig glanced up at her, she peeled down first one strap of her maillot, then the other. "My first date, and he took me up to the Stone Canyon—the local lovers' lane. He took all his dates there, which is exactly why I went out with him. He had a fifty-eight Chevy with a terrible muffler and a big back seat. I could hardly wait. Everybody else had been kissed to death, and I hadn't the least idea what they were talking about. It was...humilating. Mack was my big chance to get in on the action."

She encouraged the black maillot down her long, slender legs until it fell like a little puddle on her toes. Stepping out of the shadows, she gave the suit an impish kick in Craig's direction. The moonlight shimmered down on her bare skin like a cloak of silk. "Want to swim?"

For a big man, he could certainly move fast. His canvas shorts joined hers on the deck. "What I *want*," he growled, "is to hear what the hell happened. Keeping in mind that with *that* attitude, I'm surprised your parents didn't keep you permanently locked up."

He was aroused, she noted. They hadn't even touched, and he was...definitely, vibrantly, aroused. And coming toward her.

She took a swift step to the ladder, stepped up and around the rail, and posed for a racing dive. "Heck, he kissed like a fish," Sonia called over her shoulder. "I decided all that sex stuff was vastly overrated. Of course, when I was seventeen..." She sent one quick, teasing grin over her shoulder before diving in.

The water was cool and dark and buoyant—all delightful qualities to cool her husband off, Sonia considered. Except that his hands were cleaving through the water as if he were in the Olympics. Which would be fine, if gold medals were all he wanted to get his hands on.

And it wasn't time. His wanting to touch her wasn't enough.

She held her breath and went down, deep down, and switched directions. Evidently, she hadn't gone as deep as she planned, because their toes touched once; and she heard a garbled sound ringing through the night air when she surfaced. She was hardly about to let that slow her down. She lapped around the boat once, then twice, then a third time. Craig was by far the better swimmer but lacked the basic, purely feminine deviousness to keep changing directions on a whim.

Gasping, Sonia took the last lap around the boat and reached for the ladder. Water streamed from her body as she pulled herself up, and a quick chill trembled on her bare skin in spite of the warm night air. By the time Craig heaved himself up behind her, she was swathed in floor-length white terry cloth, all chaste and prim.

"No sharks got me," she said demurely.

"The night is young."

Unfortunately, yes, she thought sadly. The night was young and an ideal one for lovers, and Sonia managed to keep the two of them busy gathering up the telescope and pillows and whatever. Down in the cabin there were a few other little washing-up chores from dinner. Sonia showered first, and while Craig was washing the salt water off himself, she was burrowing under the covers and forcing her eyes closed and trying to make her breathing seem even.

Craig clicked open the shower door and stepped out, wrapping a towel around his waist. His pulse was racing at an odd rate. It had been racing that way all day. Sonia was the cause, and when he stepped out into their stateroom, there was a glint of something dark and unfathomable in his eyes. Torture would have been easier to handle than the teasing that Sonia had handed out all day.

At first he'd been amused by her antics. Sonia had never been predictable. He loved that in her, but sometime earlier that day his humor had died. In part, he thought she'd just been playing, enjoying the high that came with their impromptu vacation. In part, he'd been so wrapped up in his own problems that he hadn't really thought out her motivations. And in part, perhaps, after living on the ragged edge of frustration for so many weeks, he just hadn't noticed that Sonia's behavior was distinctly out of character.

Dropping the towel, he spotted her curled-up form on the bed. His pulse abruptly stopped racing. Sonia was totally still, except for the odd pattern of her breathing.

She wasn't asleep, only pretending to be.

Very quietly, he turned out the light. Instead of joining her in bed, he slipped out into the salon, closing the door behind him. Collapsing in a chair with his head thrown back, he closed his eyes.

She didn't want him to make love to her? She'd been sending him sexual S.O.S. signals all day.

It was past time he figured out what game she was playing. He felt as if he'd been kicked, hard and painfully, in the ribs. For weeks, he'd survived his own deprivation. That wasn't the same thing at all as being deprived of his right to love her, please her, touch her. A man could survive a hell of a lot longer without food than without water. And no, he wasn't in a desert.

His heart was just beginning to feel as if he were lost in one.

12

CRAIG WOKE TO find himself alone in the bed, his arms curled around a pillow. He groped for his watch on the bedside table. It was barely six. *Not* a likely hour for Sonia to be up and around—barring World War III or Christmas.

Unless she was making a distinct effort to be out of touching range whenever he was around.

Again.

Swinging his legs over the side of the bed, he broodingly tossed the pillow aside and dragged a hand through his hair. Somewhere in the distance he could hear the faint scream of gulls fishing for their breakfast. A brilliant sun was trying to peek through the opaque curtains of their cabin, and beneath his feet the boat undulated in peaceful sway.

None of that peace touched the almost violent determination inside his head. He'd gone to bed with the mood, he'd slept with it, and again awoke to the same powerful, indefinable feelings gnawing at him. He felt driven to the wall. But hadn't he driven himself there?

Impatiently, he stood up and reached for his jeans. Very few minutes later, after splashing his face with cold water and raking a brush through his hair, he stalked barefoot over the thick carpet toward the salon.

He stopped abruptly when he saw Sonia with her head buried in the refrigerator, her back to him. Silently plunging his hands into his back pockets, for a while he just

studied her. During the night, he'd come to several con-
clusions about what she was up to, which now appeared
rather useless. In a single glance, he could see very
quickly that her game plan had changed. For one thing,
she was wearing a bra, and she certainly hadn't done
that in the last thirty-six hours.

And she'd pulled on an oversized T-shirt that denied
any claim to sexiness; it was blue and wrinkled and
voluminous. Beneath it, he could just see the bottoms of
her white shorts when she bent over. Her hair was pulled
back with a terry-cloth band, and she wasn't wearing
even a touch of makeup; her skin was clear and soft and
golden, her lips their natural color.

She hadn't spotted him yet. She was too busy noisily
stirring orange juice in a pitcher with a big wooden spoon.
When that was done she yawned, a huge, lazy yawn.

For the first time in days, Craig felt a natural smile
form on his own lips.

A very complicated set of devils had been chasing
him for weeks. For an instant, they receded, and it was
as if a spring had uncoiled, a key unlocked some door.
Love, at times, could be foolishly simple. And as powerful as the pulse suddenly erratically beating in his throat.
Sonia *was* that power, and her feminine games had been
driving him nuts. Tease and withdraw, tease and withdraw—they'd *never* played those kind of games with
each other. Sonia was very subtle and had never played
such immature tricks as trying to make him jealous of
her former beaux. Exhibitionism. Chase. Tease.

If she thought she was actually getting away with
something, she was terribly...right. Every male nerve
ending would have been delighted to explode very early
last night. All night long, he'd felt on the fragile edge
of violence.

And this morning, if her choices of bulky T-shirt and
sweatband were supposed to calm anyone-in-particular's
raging libido, they had certainly failed. Her breasts were
well buried and her fanny hidden...and neither had

anything to do with the essential desirability of Sonia.
She was terribly mistaken if she thought they did.

"Craig? You're up. I thought you'd sleep in this morning." Sonia felt her heart skip a beat at the look of her
husband bearing down on her like a great sleepy brown
bear. Well. Not sleepy. She smiled a little uncertainly at the oddly intense expression radiating from his
eyes, and then turned away. "Just sit down, you. I
have a terrific breakfast planned. Melon, then ham and
eggs . . . Won't take more than a minute—it's almost
ready. Coffee and juice first . . ."

She whipped a steaming mug on the counter in front
of him, then a small glass of orange juice.

"You're up early," he commented, as he slid onto the
cushioned stool.

"The salt air," she said breezily.

"And then, you went to sleep early last night, didn't
you?"

Such an innocuous question. Amazing that she felt
instantly uneasy. "Um. Yes." She turned quickly. The
eggs were all whisked in a bowl, but she had yet to add
pepper and cheese.

"You were extremely tired."

"I certainly was," she agreed, and whisked harder.

"Yet you seemed so wide awake. After our swim."

The air in the cabin was stifling, surprising when the
windows were all open and the morning was still cool.
Craig's voice was mild. Teasing, really. There was no
reason to get nervous, she told herself. She'd woken up
nervous enough. One could play with fire only so
long . . . and then it had miraculously occurred to her that
she could get burned as well. She had in mind starting
out the day low key, easy, and . . . safe. Safe meaning
attire that couldn't possibly be a turn-on.

"Sleepiness just seemed to creep up on me all at once,"
she said hurriedly, and bounced a fork and knife on the
counter, tossing Craig a quick glance before pivoting
back to the stove. That man had gorgeous shoulders. The

hair on his chest curled every which way; it always had. And his eyes were very blue—too blue, too damned blue—for this early in the morning. She grabbed the spatula. "We've got a thousand things to do today."

"What did you have in mind?"

"Fishing, for one. We've got all the gear. And Mr. Bartholomew went on and on about the fish in these waters. Marlin and sailfish and snapper, even barracuda once we move out a little deeper. You know, though . . ." She slid his eggs on a plate and set it in front of him. "I wouldn't mind a nice red snapper for dinner. Sailfish are another thing. I don't want to risk catching one; every single time I see one mounted I get sick. They're so beautiful . . ."

"Sit down, honey. If you don't want breakfast yourself, at least have a cup of coffee."

"I forgot your melon."

"*Sit.*"

She perched obediently on the cushioned stool next to him, hugged her coffee mug in her hands, and smiled brightly. Her husband was sending out calming, soothing vibrations. Which was very strange, because she felt increasingly unnerved. "If you don't want to go fishing, we can explore the shore of the cove. We could take the dinghy. I'll row in; you can row back," she remarked magnanimously.

"You'll row *with* the surf, and I fight the battle against the tide on the way back?"

"And if you're *really* good, I'll even let you make the picnic lunch."

"One of us," Craig mentioned, "is in an awfully lazy mood this morning."

"Exactly," Sonia agreed impishly. "We can gather shells and swim and lie around in the sand. There are palm trees out there just waiting to provide a little shade. Now, it may be the coast of Texas, but who's carrying an atlas? It *looks* like the shoreline of a nice little deserted Pacific island."

Craig chuckled, pushing back his plate. He turned and swung his leg around, hooking his bare foot on the rung of her stool. He watched as Sonia ever so unobtrusively tried to shift away from any physical contact, but between his leg and the teak bar she had nowhere to go.

That very small effort at withdrawal from her aroused a very pure, very basic, very male instinctive response in him. The same instinct that had nearly driven him over the edge the night before. His jeaned calf rubbed against Sonia's bare one, and his wife's chatter accelerated just slightly, like the increased rev of a motor.

"If you don't want to do any of that, we could snorkel. There's equipment in that locker on deck."

"Yes," he agreed.

"You're supposed to be able to see all kinds of fish and things in the shallow waters."

"Yes."

Sonia could feel his eyes on her lips and throat and felt another dozen of her nerve endings zoom to life. He shouldn't be looking at her like that *now*, for heaven's sake. Couldn't he see she was dressed like a derelict? And she was *not* going to succumb to those damn eyes. Not if he had in mind more one-sided loving. She had several days of specific activities planned to ensure that his libido was hot-wired solely on his own behalf.

Furthermore, she had the sneaky feeling he was deliberately trying to make conversation difficult. With utmost grace, she stood up, only to find that his other foot had captured the rung on the opposite side of her. She was pinned in. "I'll do the dishes now," she said cheerfully.

"In a minute. Finish your coffee."

Her bottom despondently plopped back down on the stool. Nothing was going well. "Which would you like to do?" she asked brightly.

"The choices are fishing and snorkeling and picnicking on the beach in the cove?"

She picked up her mug, nodding. "Actually, we could probably do them all. We're up early."

"Very early," he agreed.

His tone was still mild. One would think he was trying to soothe a fractious kitten. Sonia was not soothed. She took another hurried sip of coffee. "And if you don't want to do any of *those* things—"

"I think you're in the mood for a very busy day."

She nodded, much more happily. It was the first sign that he was going to prove...tractable. "We take vacations so rarely. We may as well take advantage of every minute."

"I agree." Craig set down his mug. "We *should* take advantage of every minute. And I think we should do everything on your list. Tomorrow. Today we're already busy."

Her eyebrows lifted in surprise. "We're already—?"

"We're going to spend this day in bed, Sonia."

A few drops of her coffee decided to leap right out of her cup. Craig took a napkin to mop it up.

"Finish your coffee, honey," he said gently. He made every effort to keep his voice calm and soothing. It didn't seem to be working. Sonia was both nervous and clearly...not in the mood. Huge green-blue eyes peered at him over her coffee cup.

His ethical system flew out the window. His unbudgeable, rocklike, irrefutable ethical system. No one and nothing had ever made Craig do anything he believed wasn't right. And as much as he adored his Sonia, she was going to have to get in the mood. Two months of abstinence had just, very simply, combusted inside him with all the docility of nuclear fission.

Did he mean what she hoped he meant? Was he thinking of *his* pleasure for a welcome change?

Sonia licked dry lips. "Listen..."

"Finish your coffee. I want to go to bed."

Rapidly, she raised the cup to her lips again. A disgraceful feeling of utter elation was trying to swamp her.

"The first time, unfortunately, it's going to go fast," he said gently. "Not the second time. The second time, we'll take it nice and slow. Then we'll have lunch. After

lunch you can nap. And after you nap, we'll be tired of
mattresses, Sonia, and we can go for a swim. We're
going to do a complex study of friction in salt water,
body friction; it's going to be an in-depth study... You're
not drinking your coffee," he chided gently.

Hurriedly, she took another sip. Actually, she downed
the cup.

His legs hooked around the rungs of her stool; he
leaned closer with his palms spread on her thighs. "When
you bought that red bikini you wore yesterday, you must
have been in an inciting-violence kind of mood. I hate
to say this, honey, but it's your own damn fault the first
time is going to go too fast."

She nodded. Everything was her fault. She would
gladly have taken responsibility for the earth caving in.
Who cared? She hadn't heard that sound in his voice in
weeks. That unmistakable I'm-going-to-take-you tone.

"You want me to tell you how much I want you?"
His voice was gravelly, almost pained, trying to be light,
trying to be humorous.

She set down her cup. She wasn't smiling. *"Want*
me, then," she whispered vibrantly.

"How on earth could you doubt it?"

In a twinkling, he gathered her up. The stools teetered
behind them. His mouth pressed on hers as if he were
totally unaware her neck could snap from that kind of
pressure; his length to her length seared into one. Air
was forgotten. Breathing was forgotten. His hands were
running up and down her spine, his fingers finally closing
around her hips, crushing her to him.

His lips lifted from hers long enough to trail more
heated kisses on her cheeks, down to her throat. "But
what has been *wrong,* then?" Sonia whispered achingly.
"Craig..."

The T-shirt muffled her words. *Her* T-shirt. In a moment, it went soaring over her head; his palms skimmed
down her white shorts, and he lifted her to get her out
of them. She didn't argue. His lips crushed down on hers

again with a bruising pressure, a bruising sweet, sweet pleasure. So rough... Craig had never been rough. And the drowning hunger of his lips ignited a sweet, fierce hunger in her as well.

He carried her up a step and then another. She felt like laughing for the first time in weeks. The bed couldn't have been thirty feet away, that gorgeous stateroom set up with satin sheets and opaque curtains and soft pillows. But he placed her on the carpet, and through the slits in the curtains the morning sun was blinding... at least for that instant before Craig's head dipped down to hers again.

She tried to draw back for a brief gulp of air. He wouldn't let her. His tongue slid inside her parted lips, a busy, busy tongue informing her without words that she didn't need to breathe.

He was absolutely right. She needed that arrogant tongue. She needed the feel of his chest and his heartbeat crushing her breasts; she savored his impatience as he finally pulled away to peel off his jeans.

His flesh was so warm, all taut and strained, yet giving beneath her stroking palms. Such a rage of love she felt for him. His limbs were tangled with hers, oddly awkward when they'd played the game so many times. It didn't matter. His need, his desire, communicated itself to her, and she accepted his love as if it were riches. Her unselfish lover radiated desire; she invited his selfishness. Her fingers curled around him, and she rejoiced at the sound of his gasp of pleasure.

"Don't," he hissed softly. "Sonia, if you touch me—"

He would explode. The warning was implicit, but she touched him anyway. One finger lightly traced the shape of him, and then her palm curled around his pulsing warmth.

He brushed her hand away, but she felt the tremor that shook his body. His head bent, and she saw the faint sheen of moisture on his temples, that coat of sensuous

moisture like silk on his shoulders. His lips traced the
line from her throat to her breasts. Her nipples were
already taut for the wash of his tongue, yet a helpless
shiver vibrated through her when his teeth gently grazed
the sensitive flesh.

She felt a rush of sheer sexual pleasure, but that wasn't
the main cause of the trembling inside her. Mr. Hamilton
was out of control. It was about time. Only, darn it, so
was she.

Her fingertips danced over heated skin, down the muscled curve of his shoulders to his spine to his taut buttocks, finally resting on his thighs. He twisted. Such an
impatient body, such exploding need. Plush carpet pressed
into her spine, abrasive, ungiving. Sun poured on her
eyes, and she lowered her lids. The flesh of his neck
was so vulnerable; her lips whispered over it, so very
gently; her teeth nuzzled, so very gently...

"Sonia, if you don't stop..."

She had no intention of stopping. The damn boat was
welcome to sink. Her lover was back. For some crazy
reason, his lips were sinking from breasts to ribs to navel.
The silly man was obviously still concerned with *her*
pleasure.

"Come to me," she whispered throatily. "Craig, I want
my legs around you; I want to feel you inside me. Don't
wait. Don't wait..."

For an instant, the searing images exploded in his
head again. The man with light eyes, the darkness, that
instant when Sonia's eyes sought him out, desperately
wanting and needing and expecting him to save her, that
instant when he'd never felt more impotent, more helpless, his failure... The images were real; they had been
real for weeks, as real as if it had all just happened.

"*No,*" Sonia whispered fiercely. "You're not doing
that to me again, dammit. Or to yourself. Look at me,
Craig."

Her palms framed the sides of his face. She wanted
to kiss away that terrible look in his eyes. Frustration

and desire and all the fierce feelings of love she had for him glowed in her eyes.

There was one moment... but then a smile formed on his lips. That smile hovered and came closer, until with exquisite tenderness his mouth molded itself to hers. Even as her arms tightened around him, he was shifting his body over hers; in a surging thrust they were one again.

So long... too long. Her legs locked around him, terrified he would leave her.

There was nothing to be afraid of. A low groan escaped her lips as Craig urged them both to a fierce, pulsing rhythm. She could feel the hunger in him as if it were a live thing. His skin was damp with it; his eyes burned with it; his body shuddered with it.

"I *love* you," he whispered. "So much, so much, so much..."

At her sudden fevered cry, he felt the agony of his own release explode inside of her. Like a prisoner set free, he saw the brightness of sun behind his eyes, a world renewed in loving, all guilt banished to another time.

"One can carry laziness just a little too far, you know," Craig teased.

"It's your fault I have all the energy of a marshmallow." She parted her lips again.

Craig forked in another tidbit of steak. "Would you like me to chew it for you?" he asked gravely.

"Would you?"

"Doubtful."

"I'll settle for being fed, then." She settled back with her head back against a bunched-up blanket, surveying her husband with limpid eyes.

Two hours before, it had taken more work to unhook the dinghy from the cruiser than it had to row in to shore. By then a velvet night had fallen, so black and soft that it looked almost as crushable as fabric. They had rowed across the cove to a deserted sandy beach; undoubtedly there was civilization somewhere close by, but there were no signs of it. Palms and tropical brush guarded their privacy, and the crackling driftwood fire Craig had built on the sand tossed up delightfully colorful sparks to the sky. That steady splish-splash of surf only added to her already somnolent state.

"Open," Craig instructed.

She opened. Somewhere in the mound of sour cream on the fork was a tiny morsel of baked potato. Her wry smile made her husband chuckle, totally unrepentant at stuffing her unmercifully with the delectable goodies. "No more," she pleaded when she had swallowed the bite of potato and sour cream.

"Nonsense."

"The dinghy will sink."

"I keep hearing all these dire predictions about your getting fat. I have yet to see one spare ounce of flesh develop."

"I'm hardly going to wait until I'm waddling and you're driven into the arms of some skinny yacht owner."

Craig set aside the paper plate and sank down next to her. "I thought we'd established that she was pockmarked and wore braces."

"We haven't *established* anything." She rearranged the blanket so there was pillow potential for both heads. Two pairs of cut-off-denim-clad legs stretched out, all four sets of toes digging in the sand. "The only thing the prosecution is really aware of," Sonia said sleepily, "is that the man knows too much about boats. The rest has been simply brilliant deduction on my part. How long did you date her, anyway?"

Craig lifted his foot and sprinkled her ankle with a layer of sand. "How long have you had this violently jealous streak?" he remarked conversationally.

"Ages."

"You've kept it very well hidden."

"Thank you."

"I like it. That you're jealous."

"I'm glad that you're glad that I'm jealous," Sonia said patiently. "How long did you date her?"

He chuckled, rolling over on his stomach. His rear end, Sonia noted with amusement, was covered with sand. So was she, almost everywhere. The blanket made, at best, a crumpled pillow, and the grainy sand had crept inside her cutoffs . . . and she was amazingly, thoroughly comfortable.

But then, her husband was relaxed, as he hadn't been in weeks. His hair was disheveled, and his eyes were full of humor, and every limb and muscle reflected lazy, sated easiness. She reached over to push back a shock of hair from his forehead. "Answer me," she demanded, but her tone was loving.

"About what?"

She sighed. It was useless to pursue. "You're very good at keeping secrets, you know," she scolded.

"Only at keeping secrets you really don't want to know."

"True." Sonia added softly, "Sometimes, Craig. Not always." She stroked back that shock of hair again. This time, her fingertips lingered on his temples. "I don't need to know about your past love affairs," she said softly. "That's not part of *our* lives."

His lips pressed a kiss into the center of her palm. She closed her eyes for a moment, savoring the tender gesture, reminded of the loving they had shared all day. When her lashes fluttered open again, Craig was shifting to lean closer to her. Her palm stroked the wall of his chest.

"Craig?"

His eyes lifted to hers.

"Certain secrets you *don't* have the right to keep," she said gently. "And I think it's way past time you told me what's been bothering you."

13

SONIA SLOWLY SHIFTED to a sitting position, drawing her knees up and wrapping her arms around them. For a moment, she stared into the dying driftwood fire, wondering why on earth it was so hard to ask one very simple question of a man she knew so well and loved and trusted so very much. Pride? Her eyes raised to Craig's, to his still features and dark, brooding eyes. Pride mattered, yet one of them had to let loose of it or they'd never get past that silence. "You haven't wanted to make love with me for some weeks," she said quietly.

He expelled a suddenly restless breath. "There hasn't been a time from the first moment I met you that I haven't wanted to make love with you," he denied roughly. "Sonia . . ."

"You satisfied *my* needs. Not your own." Sonia brushed a trembling strand of hair from her cheek, looking down. "Someone very close to me taught me that satisfaction and intimacy aren't at all the same thing. Intimacy," she said quietly, "takes two. You've taught me that over four years of marriage, Craig." She was not surprised when her husband suddenly lurched to a standing position and started kicking sand on the fire. He didn't want to talk about it.

"I've thought it had something to do with Chicago," Sonia probed gently. "I wasn't sure. I'm *still* not sure of that, except that you've obviously changed since then. Doing very silly things like assuming I needed George to help me pick out my lingerie. Like paying someone to find some stupid kid a zillion miles away who can't possibly touch us again." She added softly, "Hear me?"

"Let's go back to the boat," he said swiftly.

Reluctantly, she rose, dusting the sand from the seat of her jeans. Her eyes never left Craig, as he finished packing up their dinner debris and carting it over to the dinghy. In very few minutes, Craig was dragging the little boat into the water.

She didn't have much choice but to hustle over to it. Her toes splashed in the cool, frothing surf as she helped him tug the boat farther out. In knee-deep water, the little boat was finally free floating, and Craig held it steady while she climbed in.

She studied his profile as he got in after her. His features were all stark silver and dark hollows by moonlight, his eyes unreadable, the emotions on his face stubbornly hidden in shadows.

"Let me row," she suggested.

"I don't mind."

"Really, I'd like to."

He handed her the oars, a terrible mistake on his part. Sonia swiftly rowed away from the shore and into deeper waters. Secured in their oarlocks, the wooden paddles were easy enough to maneuver. When their dinghy was far out in the cove, she abruptly raised the dripping oars and swung them into the boat.

"Sonia."

"There happen to be two of us in this marriage," she reminded him. She said it gently, but she was tempted to unlock the oars and toss them overboard. In time, he'd talk. Or they'd starve somewhere in the middle of the Gulf of Mexico.

The moon shone down on the cove; the water reflected a sudden slash of a smile on his face brought on by the fire in her eyes. "I love you," he said softly.

The tone was warm enough to melt steel. She could have killed him. He knew damn well she wasn't steel.

"I love you, too," she said with equal fervor, and reached for the starboard oarlock.

Startled, his hand snatched at hers just before she'd freed the oar to go drifting to Timbuktu. "Dammit." He took a breath, staring at her. One by one, he pried her fingers from the oar. "God, you're stubborn," he remarked.

She was silent. They stared at each other, and Sonia felt a certain sadness. She couldn't think of a time they'd pitted their equally strong wills against each other. They'd never had to before. That Craig's was often the stronger she already knew. Unfortunately, he knew her very little if he didn't recognize she was fully capable of digging in her heels when life called for it.

The oars flopped noisily inside the boat as he set them down. He leaned back, his arms stretched out along the wooden gunwales of the boat. His eyes never once left hers. "When you break a vow," he finally said quietly, "it isn't an easy thing to mend again."

"You have never broken a promise to me," she said fiercely.

He shook his head. "Dammit, don't defend me."

The boat was adrift; neither one of them seemed to notice or care. A dark night greeted them, waters that stretched in endless darkness, and Sonia waited, so very angry with him that she was hurting with it. *Talk to me*, she wanted to cry, and instead she waited longer.

"That love, honor, and cherish vow. The part about the cherish," Craig clipped out. "Corny stuff, Sonia. Only I was raised on just that corny stuff. I was raised to believe that a man keeps what he has by protecting it, by guarding it. You fight to get what you want, and then you fight to keep it." His voice abruptly softened. "You happen to be a most precious part of me, Sonia. And the problem was never what *you* expected of me but what *I* expected of myself."

Confused, she stared at his stark features.

"I *exposed* you to danger. You could have been—"

"No." Her tone was swift and sure.

"*Yes. I* hurt you. No one else. Not some fool with stringy blond hair, not some gang of hoodlums. *I* did it. I broke my vow to protect you..."

She took up the oars, too shaken to sit still. The wooden paddles sliced neatly through the waters, and she ached inside, feeling the strain on the muscles in her shoulders, feeling the pain of the man across from her.

He was so very foolish, her lover. He was a man to the core, a capital *M* man. How on earth could he ever have doubted it? "That's why," she asked quietly, "you didn't want to make love to me?"

"I kept seeing the bastard's face..." Craig roughly shifted forward, grabbing the oars. "Whenever I touched you, I saw his face, and then yours, vulnerable and terrified. We were all but making love when it happened, in that park. The only thing on my mind at that time was getting you in bed. Maybe if I'd spent a minute less time selfishly obsessed with my own needs—"

"You think you were the only one too busy fooling around to see anything else?" Sonia whispered.

Craig said nothing.

"I was the one who insisted we shake off our bodyguard, as I remember. Not you."

He still said nothing.

Her jaw firmed, and her voice was suddenly threaded with urgency. "There is nothing to blame yourself for, dammit. We *both* shook that idiotic shadow, and we *both* chose to neck in the park. Whatever went wrong, we *share* that responsibility. For that matter, I never expected or wanted you to be some kind of macho wrestler, you fool. There were five men in that gang of muggers, Craig! The worst part of the whole thing for me wasn't those goons, but seeing you unconscious in the grass. I thought..." Her voice broke.

He couldn't stand the aching threat of tears in her voice. "You can continue shouting at me," he remarked gravely, "but if you don't sit down, you're going to tip over the boat."

"I don't care." But she sank back down on the seat

with a reluctant smile. The beast. If he'd done anything but tease her, she would undoubtedly have burst out crying.

"I don't have the least idea where we are," he continued mildly.

"Neither do I."

"And I don't see any point in continuing to argue when we'd both rather go back to the yacht and make love." Craig shifted forward, planted a shaky kiss on her lips, and then put both her hands on the oars. "You row, woman. I have every reason to want to save my strength. You've already exhausted me twice today."

Sonia dragged one oar in an arc through the water until the dinghy was turned around and headed back for their cruiser. She leaned toward Craig with the forward motions and away from him as she brought the oars back. Amazing how such action echoed other, more sensual rhythms.

Her eyes rested on Craig's face, studying him pensively. He was leaned back, studying her with equal intensity, a very stark, very male, very hungry sexual promise in his eyes. He was very clearly through talking. He was willing to communicate further about the last lonely weeks, but in other ways.

The ache in her lower body said she'd already been well loved that day. She didn't need sex. She did, however, need to see that look in his eyes again. She needed that sweet, monumental relief of knowing they'd talked, that there had never been anything so terribly wrong that they couldn't solve it together.

Dip and pull, dip and pull. Craig motioned his willingness to take the oars; she shook her head.

A kind of silence gripped her, deep inside, absorbing what he'd tried to tell her. Not the words, but the guilt behind them. That he'd blamed himself for wanting her too damn much on a very still, very seductive night in Chicago . . . that he'd linked that to his right to make love to her . . . that he'd suffered through a very masculine feeling of failure to protect her—how could she not have known?

Dip and pull, dip and pull. Always, the man had bolstered and encouraged and abetted every feminine instinct in her. She felt secure about herself as a woman because of him. It had never occurred to her that Craig could possibly doubt himself as a man, or that she could have been so totally oblivious to how important that male role was in their relationship. To him.

She was suddenly very definitely in the mood to make love again. She had a great deal to show Craig about how she thought of him as a man. A great many imaginative experiments to try that would reinforce that welling love she felt, that would make very clear that they were equal mates in bed, equally sensitive, equally giving, equally . . .

Leaning forward, she handed Craig the oars. She had no more time to risk getting all tuckered out. Not when there was a long night ahead, and their cruiser was finally within sight again.

Stepping off the plane with Craig just behind her, Sonia scanned the airport crowd for a cigar-smoking, wizened little man with a wrinkled face.

Charlie found the two of them first; Sonia's cherry-red dress was impossible to miss. He whipped the cigar out of his mouth as he ambled forward. "Didn't think the two of you were ever coming back. Well, how was it?"

Charlie bent a little forward. Not that he was expecting or even wanted a peck on the cheek from Sonia, but she usually insisted on these things. He received a resounding buss and hug besides. Beaming, he grabbed for her flight bag and reached around to hook an arm across Craig's shoulder. "Looking good, you two. I can hardly wait to hear about the whole trip. You catch any good fish?"

"Not a one," Craig admitted.

"Not *one?* How could you possibly be anywhere

near"—someone bumped into him; he maneuvered aside—"that incredible fishing territory and not catch a single fish?"

"Nothing was biting, actually," Sonia said, and added swiftly, "How're the pups?"

Charlie gave her a disgusted look, as the three angled through the crowd to the baggage area. "Don't ask."

"Okay."

"They tipped over the trash. One teethed on the patio furniture. Another decided he was going to whine outside the door the *whole night*. Thinks he's going to be a lap dog, that one. John called from work," Charlie mentioned to Craig.

"Hmm?"

"John. Work. Another problem with that guy from Radoil—"

Charlie watched, amused, as Craig leaned over his wife and kissed her. The kiss wasn't long; it wasn't short either. Sonia was wearing a hat, a wide-brimmed white thing with a red ribbon; she had to hold it on with one hand. And when Craig disappeared into the getting-luggage crowd, she was still staring after him, a faint flush on her cheeks, her fingers still holding the silly hat.

Charlie cleared his throat. "So you didn't do much fishing," he chortled.

Sonia twirled in his direction, a delightful smile on her lips, almost as red as her dress. "Pardon?"

"Did you at least see the Gulf? Port-to-port it between marinas?"

"Well . . . sort of."

"Meet a lot of people?"

"Not really."

"Get a lot of swimming in then?"

"We *did* swim. We swam a lot," she assured him. "Every day."

"Somehow I thought the two of you'd be browner than you are. Not that you weren't plenty tanned when you left home, but after four days of nothing but sun—"

"It rained," Sonia improvised swiftly.

Charlie's eyebrows innocently vaulted up. "That's strange. I watched the weather report every day; the whole area was supposed to be hot and dry."

"The Gulf gets sudden rains." Sonia's eyes nervously sought Craig's lean form in the crowd. "Lots of them. You'd be surprised."

"That's a shame," Charlie commiserated.

"It was," Sonia agreed.

"Nothing to do on a boat in the rain."

"We played," Sonia assured him, "a lot of chess."

Charlie's most undignified guffaw startled her. Craig shot her a questioning glance as he returned with their two small bags. Charlie grabbed both, adjusted them with the flight bag he'd already claimed, and stumbled ahead of the two of them, still chuckling.

"I've missed him," Sonia remarked to Craig as he steered her toward the exit with his palm at her back. "I could kill him, but I always miss him when we're away."

"Pardon? I can't hear you because of that hat."

She lifted her head, holding the hat in place again, an amused smile softening her lips. "That doesn't make rational sense, Mr. Hamilton, that you can't hear because of a hat. Give us another."

"All right." He took advantage, bending down again to test his lips against hers. The taste was not appreciably different than it had been moments ago. Delicious. The taste of her wasn't any different, and the feel of her wasn't any different, but after four days of seeing Sonia naked most of the time, he was having trouble adjusting to his lady fully clothed. The cherry-red linen dress and absurd hat and red and white shoes, the flick of mascara on her lashes again, the lingering hint of perfume . . . he liked it all. And wanted it all off again as soon as possible.

His lips lingered, until Sonia pulled back with a sassy frown. "You will behave yourself in the airport. That's the second time in five minutes."

"Then let's get home."

But arriving home was so complicated. Charlie talked

continuously; the pups demanded attention; Craig had
ninety-nine phone calls to return; they had to eat; her
mother called; Charlie talked some more...Charlie refused to stop talking. Sonia had to give him three lem-
onades and tell him countless stories about rainy afternoons
before he finally got up to leave around nine, still chuckling.

"What is *wrong* with him tonight?" Sonia demanded
irritably.

"He's on to us." Craig switched off the light in the
kitchen, then trailed Sonia through the hall. "It might
have helped if you hadn't handed him that cock-and-bull
story about rainstorms."

She unzipped her dress as she walked down the dark
hall. "He seemed to expect us to have caught five million
fish. What was I supposed to do? Tell him what we really
did for four days?"

In their bedroom, Craig flicked on the dresser lamp,
and Sonia savored for an instant the feeling of being
home. The Wyoming sun, the car ride through dusty
hills, the coming home and the look of the ranch and the
feeling of total relaxation didn't seep through her until
her eyes lit on the familiar beamed ceiling and corner
fireplace and familiar furnishings of their bedroom.

Her dress slipped to the floor. She picked it up and
wandered toward the closet, her slim form clad in a pale
blue satin slip. Behind the closet door, she slipped off
her heels and pantyhose, and then peered unobtrusively
around the edge of the door.

Craig's shirt was already draped over a chair, and
he'd removed his shoes and socks. He was still wearing
pale gray pants and his eyes were waiting for her and
she loved him totally. They'd had four days to renew
loving. They hadn't wasted a single moment.

"Come out of there."

"You're exhausted and you know it. Quit sound-
ing...impatient," she ordered him.

"I *am* impatient."

"You couldn't be. We were darn near late for the plane because of you!"

"That was hours ago."

"Honestly. A teenage boy at a drive-in movie has more control than you do." Sonia emerged from the recesses of the closet wearing her best prim and proper expression.

It was difficult to hold the pose when Craig all but tackled her. His arms snatched her high, like booty; an instant after that her spine bounced on the mattress and Craig followed, his weight unmercifully heavy on top of her.

"Up, you oaf," she ordered breathlessly.

Craig shifted his leg, the one that was in danger of cutting off the circulation in her thigh. His head dipped down, his lips nuzzling at her throat. Just between her collarbones was a little private hollow where her pulse beat out a rhythm when she was aroused.

She was aroused. He was aroused.

It was all her fault. He thought he'd had it all. He hadn't, obviously. Sonia had turned into an irresistibly uninhibited, wanton vixen the last few days. He had the feeling she'd planned some farfetched seductions when she'd signed on for that little cruise, but there was no real explaining the explosive lovemaking that had erupted between them. There was something faintly sinful over falling in love with his wife again after all this time. Particularly when he'd never fallen out of love with her to begin with.

His teeth nipped at her shoulder. "You called me an oaf. Sweetheart, you're going to pay for that."

"Darn," she said with mock unhappiness.

"You'll be sorry," he assured her.

He uncurled one leg from her, simply because he couldn't get her slip off otherwise. He hadn't seen her so burdened with clothes in days. There was still more. One lacy pale blue bra that was see-through, he noted as he held it up to the light. Then one pair of pale blue panties that were also see-through, and had a ribbon in the silliest place.

Sonia snatched the panties from him and tossed them on the floor. "They were on sale."

"An X-rated sale."

The only way to wipe the smile from his lips was to unsnap his pants. He darned well made the zipper impossible to undo. He just refused to get out of the way; his lips were pressed full on hers and both his palms were trying to claim her breasts, and those breasts were already painfully swollen...

There was something sinful about falling in love with one's husband again when one had never fallen out of love with him to begin with. Sin was so nice.

And Craig was the devil. He'd always been an imaginative lover; somehow he'd managed to drag out of her the most liquid, new, almost frightening responses...

His lips tugged on one nipple, and then he left her. Standing next to the bed, he shrugged off the rest of his clothes. He took endless more seconds crossing the room to turn off the light.

"Craig—"

He turned the light back on. "All of a sudden, you have to see every little thing," he complained. "Who's going to have the energy to turn off the light afterward?"

"You will."

"We won't argue about it," he said amicably.

He dropped back on the mattress, but it was a big mattress, and for the moment he didn't touch her. For the moment he just took in the fevered brightness in her eyes, the glow of lamplight on her bare skin, the rapid rise and fall of her breasts. Those breasts tapered to such a tiny waist. Legs stretched endlessly from there.

He knew every inch of the territory. He knew the quiver that touched her spine when his lips pressed against her thigh; he knew the sudden restlessness that ached through her body when he held her against him, length to length. He knew the tension that gripped her like strange fever when he pressed his arousal against her, announcing his intention. His intention was to take her. To claim her. To possess her. Hard and fast.

When he got around to it.

Sonia was perceptive, and gentle and passionate and loving. The last few days he'd willingly forgotten the ghosts that had haunted him. Sonia was a delightful ghost chaser. Whatever had possessed him to think he could not make love with his wife hadn't stood a chance.

In another realm, though, their renewed physical relationship had only intensified certain feelings he had. He loved her, coveted her, cherished her. His protective instincts were ten times more acute than they had ever been. He wanted to weave a silken web around her, to protect her laughter and her softness and the brimming happiness on her face...

Sonia trembled, feeling his arms reach for her, enfold her, wrap her up against his hard, taut body. Her breasts pressed into his chest; her legs tightened around him. He murmured soft love words in her ear; she couldn't hear over the wild, sweet thundering of her heart. As he shifted over her, she welcomed him into the core of her, her body surging to meet his with supreme urgency. So rich, so rich...

Nothing could mar it. She felt the incredible power of woman within her, the power to snare her mate, the richness of giving him back the power of manhood. She felt full to brimming, sexually climbing still higher on one level, lovingly soaring past endless skies on another.

He exploded within her only seconds after she'd reached the same delicious release. The silence afterward was like the sweet tumbling down of a soft spring rain, all hush and peace. He held on, staying inside her, as her arms remained wrapped around him.

Her damp cheek rested in the curve of his shoulder. Her husband, her lover, her mate... The world was fine, she knew she would sleep well tonight. Brimming with well-being, she pressed a smile on his chest as a kiss. A stranger had frightened her those long weeks past. Not a man in a park from a forgotten night, but her husband.

He was a stranger no more. She felt secure and safe and sure again.

"Sonia?" He tried to shift; she wouldn't budge. He pressed a lazy kiss at her throat. "I'm too heavy," he murmured.

"You just stay right where you are," she murmured back.

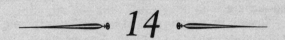

14

"HAVE YOU SEEN Marina?" Sonia asked her friend's secretary cheerfully.

The blonde shook her head with a rueful smile. "She's been everywhere this morning. You could check downstairs; one shipment was all mixed up—darn it. I know she was expecting you, Mrs. Hamilton . . ."

"That's all right." Sonia swept past, turned the corner into Marina's office, and viewed the turbulent chaos with an affectionate grin. After plopping a half-dozen fabric samples on the floor, she found a seat; after plopping another dozen files neatly next to them, she established a footstool, and settled back in comfort with a magazine.

A five-foot whirlwind wafted in shortly thereafter with cinnamon hair wisping wildly around her face and glasses propped on top of her head. Marina took one look at Sonia and groaned. "God, take that glow off your face. I can't stand people looking that happy anywhere around me. I take it the vacation was a good one?"

"Terrific." Sonia chuckled. "Where's your coffee machine?"

"It used to be two doors down. But it's probably broken. Everything has broken or gone wrong today. There's no reason why that should be any different."

"Cream or sugar?"

"I tell you it can't be working."

Sonia returned a few moments later with two Styrofoam cups of coffee. Marina had thrown herself some-

165

where behind the mounds of paperwork on her desk; Sonia peered over the stacks before setting one steaming cup down.

"Don't start," Marina warned. "If I were a little less chintzy, I'd probably get some extra help around here. But don't think I don't know where everything is." Marina gulped some of the hot brew and settled back with a sigh. "I've had better days."

"I get that feeling."

"That glow is still on your face," Marina said glumly, glaring at Sonia as she settled back in the chair. "And no one but you would have dared put those colors together."

Sonia chuckled. Her pale violet jumpsuit had had a drab look to it, until she found a pair of violet and leaf-green sandals, then added a leaf-green rope necklace and belt. In bright colors, the blend wouldn't have worked, but in pastels the two were eye-catching.

The glow came far more naturally, and like a smug cat with cream, Sonia knew it was there. They'd been home from their four-day cruise for a week. And all that week happiness had been free, like a gift.

"I refuse to ask if you've made any decision about the job, because I can't take another setback today," Marina informed her. "So we'll just drink our coffee. I want to hear about every detail of that vacation of yours; then you will listen to me rant until I calm down—"

"I think I will take the job, if you can live with my terms," Sonia said mildly.

"If that place in Dayton sends me one more batch of mismatched sizes, I'm going to—" Marina set down her coffee cup and leaned forward, skeptical eyes rivited on Sonia. "*Terms* I can live with. My husband, not always," she drawled deadpan. "Let's hear it. I even forgive you for being beautiful."

Sonia burst out laughing. "I'm serious, darn it."

"And I'm listening." Marina's blue eyes abruptly got a shrewd look in them. Business was business, after all.

"I want to set up your consulting corner, just as we talked about it. I'll set it up, organize it, staff it, and keep a long nose in on your buying choices," Sonia said frankly. She leaned back in the chair, her chin on her knuckles. "So far not too bad?"

"I'm waiting for the bad part."

"I think I could get the whole project rolling before your fall clothes come in," Sonia said musingly, "if you'd allow a little extra budget for some additional costs."

"Expected."

Sonia nodded. "But from there, I want a part-time supervisory role, Marina," she said quietly. "I've thought about it. I believe it *can* be set up to function well with the proper staff. After that, I would love to be involved, but only if you want me on a part-time basis."

"I want you on any basis, you nitwit. You chose half my spring line as it was, talking over coffee." Marina shot her a disappointed look, half resigned. "Why not more?"

"Babies," Sonia said honestly.

"Babies?"

"You know. They usually come in six- to eight-pound packages. Not house-trained, hairless, toothless; there's really very little to redeem the little . . ."

Marina's eyes were suddenly twinkling. "Oh, God. You haven't fallen for that game?"

"I'd tell you I was nine days pregnant, but you'd call me a fool." Sonia grinned impishly, her cheek still cupped in her palm. "Shut up, Marina. I can see by the expression on your face . . . Anyway, I've got a few months ahead where I can work like the devil, and then a few months where I'm hoping I'll be so bloated and ugly and fat that I won't want to venture out of the house. Although, if not . . ."

"I would love to see you bloated and ugly and fat," Marina remarked. "Knowing Craig, I expect he would, too. Have a busy vacation, did you?"

"I came here to talk business," Sonia said severely.

Marina slid her glasses back on top of her head. "We can negotiate your leave of absence over lunch."

Sonia stepped out of the Rabbit and stretched, surprised to see Craig's car parked in the drive. It was only two in the afternoon, hours before he normally returned from work. Her lips curled in an anticipatory smile as she bent over the back seat to snatch up her packages.

Tawny Lady came bounding toward her as Sonia slammed the car door. Chuckling, she rapidly tried to maneuver the packages to protect herself against a very long, very wet wagging tail. "You've been swimming," Sonia scolded. "Now, you know I'll pet you, but you'll have to wait until I change my clothes."

Sonia sighed at the limpid, pleading eyes and exuberant tail and extended her hand. Immediately, a very wet shaggy head nuzzled beneath it, content with just that moment's contact before the bitch spotted a rabbit— undoubtedly imaginary—in the brush and took off again. Sonia stared at her wet palm, shook it, and gingerly maneuvered her way toward the house, under the burden of packages.

The kitchen was blessedly cool, and silent. "Craig?" Setting her packages on the counter, Sonia turned on the faucet and rinsed her hands. As she was drying them, an impish smile creased her features, and she reached into the cupboard for two glasses. A gin and tonic seemed an adequate welcome for a husband home early, even if it was still the middle of the day.

Carrying the glasses through the hall a few minutes later, Sonia glanced into the living room and then passed through to the bedroom, taking a tiny sip from her drink. She smiled. Craig's was the actual gin and tonic; hers was the tonic with lots of fresh lime; she'd never had a real liking for hard liquor. Craig had always teased her for referring to her favorite drink as a G & T . . .

Her eyes widened in surprise as she paused in the bedroom doorway. A suitcase was on the bed, half filled.

Craig stepped out of the bathroom, dressed in gray suit pants and white shirt, a tie hung loosely around his neck, and he was holding a shaving kit. She'd sent an extremely relaxed, well-rested man to work, and he'd returned strained and exhausted. A pallor cloaked his tan, and his eyes were stone-hard and dark blue. A tense, determined purpose marked every movement he made.

Surprise yielded to instant empathy. She surged forward, set down her drink and handed him his, as she took the shaving kit from his hands. "I'll do that. Darn it. What happened? Where are you going this time?"

It had happened before, though not often. The extraction process that Craig had developed was new and experimental. Problems cropped up quickly in the oil business, and solving them always seemed to be complicated, expensive, and exhausting. He'd made a trip to Atlanta one time and another to northern California, and Craig was invariably crabby when travel and trouble went together.

Sonia viewed the jumble of shirts in the suitcase with a sigh that was amused in spite of her concern. The man couldn't pack worth a damn. His shirts inevitably looked like wrinkled raisins, and he never remembered socks. "Jeans or suits?" she asked efficiently, and glanced back with a warm supportive smile.

Her eyebrows lifted just a little when he didn't return her smile. Craig's eyes glowed into hers, bright blue and tense; there was a *watchfulness* about him. Abruptly, he turned to the closet, drawing out yet more shirts.

"Hey," she murmured teasingly, confused by the steadfast stare. Determination radiated from him like a quiet menace, and when he'd shifted his eyes from hers she felt an uneasy lurch in her stomach.

"I have to go to Chicago, Sonia. Only for a few days. Not long, I promise you."

Such a gentle, gentle voice. Her heart flipped over again. "I'll do that," she insisted, taking the shirts from his hand, but her voice suddenly wavered. She motioned him to the chair with all the authority of an old-fashioned schoolmarm trying to win a smile.

She didn't win one. As she bent over his suitcase, her hands automatically started refolding his shirts. "What on earth is happening in Chicago?" she asked. "Your work hasn't taken you there before."

"They've found him, Sonia."

Her head slowly lifted. How she wished she had no idea what he was talking about! Amazing how fast an absolutely perfect world could come tumbling down. The joy and exhilaration since they'd been home, her rash, almost ridiculous confidence that the two of them were fine again, that Craig was fine, her busy, heel-clicking day . . .

"Sit down, honey." Craig took from her hands the shirt she'd folded three times. The quick brand of his lips on her forehead was meant to be reassuring. His mouth was firm and warm and roughly swift. No apologies offered. "The man's name is Tim Rawler. He was picked up on another mugging charge," Craig said grimly. "Only this time, he managed to kill someone. The cop who was trying to catch him in the act."

Sonia's eyes followed him.

"There's no question it's the same man." He tossed underwear on top of the suitcase, then a belt. "The police wired his picture to me. I just got it after lunch." He flicked another glance at his wife. Aquamarine eyes were staring at him, far more brilliant than a gem. She was standing awkwardly in the middle of the room, one hand clutching her upper arm as if she were suddenly cold. "Sonia . . ."

"Are you saying they have him behind bars?" she questioned carefully. Even to her own ears, her voice sounded hollow.

"They have him behind bars," Craig agreed.

"Then there's no reason at all for you to go. If they've got him on a murder charge . . ."

His jaw tightened. "I knew that was exactly how you'd

feel..." He took a weary breath. "And I knew you'd want me just to forget it. I can't do that, honey. It isn't that simple..."

"It *is*, Craig. He'll be up for life if he killed a policeman. They don't need *us*." Her voice took on an impassioned note. "There is no reason for either of us to be involved anymore. *None*."

"I'm going," he said patiently, "to press charges. People get off on technicalities all the time. Maybe it really *is* an open-and-shut case, but I won't take that chance." He snapped the suitcase closed and swung it down to the carpet. "I can't." Still moving swiftly, he crossed to the dresser to take a swallow of the drink Sonia had brought him. Their eyes met in the mirror—his as unyielding as steel, hers furious.

"It's not that I don't care. Do you think I want anyone else victimized by him?" She shook her head once and then again and then wildly shook it still another time. "I don't, Craig, but I never want to hear about that man again; I never want to hear anything about that incident again. It's *over* for us, and it's done every bit of damage to our lives that it's going to do."

"It *is* over," Craig agreed swiftly. "I'll handle whatever else has to be handled. You won't have to say a word, be involved in any way—"

"That is *not* the point."

Craig's tone turned iron, his don't-push-me voice, rarely, rarely used but always unmistakable. "There is no way in *hell* I'm going to let that man get away with hurting you, without *seeing*, without *knowing* that he's paying for it."

"That's it, isn't it? What you really want to do is punch the man out, settle some score. It's some *male* thing for you, Craig, but dammit, what about the two of us?"

An almost ashen color crept over his bronze skin. "I love you," he said in a low voice, "more than my life." The words were so simply, so quietly said that she couldn't believe it when he picked up the suitcase. "The plane leaves at four. I can barely get there on time as it is. When I get back—"

"Craig, he's a *stranger*," she tried desperately. "You've let a stranger all but tear us apart, and for how long now? It's still happening. You really think if you find some way to hurt him back that it would solve something? *What* would it solve?" She took a breath, her voice dropping down two shaky octaves. "Everything that matters to us is right here. There's *nothing* you can do in Chicago. *Nothing.* And if you really can't see that—"

"Don't," he snapped bitterly, "say something you don't mean."

"Then don't you walk out that door!"

For a moment, his eyes bored into hers, and then he was gone.

He was *gone.*

Sonia stood stock-still, her heart hammering so hard that she couldn't think. She winced when she heard the sound of a distant door slamming. She could taste blood on her lip, from the unconscious bite of soft lip between teeth.

Her palms edged up and down her bare arms, seeking warmth, finding none. She could not remember ever having been so terribly cold.

He'd accused her of not being able to understand. The problem was, she *did* understand. His feelings about himself as a man were tied up in all those macho values he'd grown up with. A man must always be strong; he must protect the weak; he must guard his woman. Oh, she knew.

He wanted to protect her from a stranger, because some macho man would have proven his masculinity with his fists.

She wanted protection from her man. Protection from the aching loneliness she felt now, the terrible gnawing

emptiness of wondering how their love suddenly meant
less to him than what he "had to do."

She stared, heartsick, at the silent open door. The
whole house echoed a stillness, a yawning quiet. Somewhere inside her she was angry, and hurt was trying to
explode in the unshed tears in her eyes, but more than
that she felt simply . . . afraid. No matter what he thought,
Craig had not failed her in Chicago. It was *now* she felt
vulnerable, and terribly alone.

15

FROM THE CORNER of the couch in the dark living room, Sonia heard the sound of an opened door. "What's going on around here?" Charlie bellowed. "Not a single light. Not a . . . ouch!"

A light went on in the kitchen; she could see the square of yellow in the open doorway and forced herself to uncurl from her position on the couch. Roughly, she pushed back her hair and moved toward the kitchen.

"Sorry, Charlie, I . . ."

Charlie pivoted from his crouched stance by the open refrigerator, a growing furrow on his brow as he caught a glimpse of her. "Why didn't you call me if you were sick? Where's Craig?"

"I'm not sick," she immediately assured him. She moved forward, feeling disoriented and exhausted and frightened. The clock over the stove said it was six. She seemed to have lost four hours. Her heart was tied up in knots . . . but she had to feed Charlie. How could she have forgotten him? And at least for a few minutes, she could forget that horrible argument and at least *do* something. "Craig had to go away. Unexpectedly. He'll be back in a few days. Listen, I had planned to grill some pork chops, but I . . ."

"What the hell is wrong?"

"*Nothing* is wrong," she said succinctly, and opened the refrigerator. "I forgot to start the grill. It won't take more than a minute or two—" She took two long breaths. "George was having trouble with the colt this morning,

174

wasn't he? I saw the vet's car here before I went into town."

"Sonia," Charlie said softly. "Honey, exactly where is Craig?"

"In Chicago," Sonia said brightly. "He'll be back in a day or two." She wouldn't upset Charlie for the world, and she *knew* her voice sounded cheerful. Unfortunately, tears chose just that moment to drop from her eyes. Plop, plop, plop, all over the potatoes as she sliced them, all over the chops as she took them out of the refrigerator . . .

She fled to the outdoor gas grill and turned it on. When her eyes were dry again, she went back inside, closing the glass doors behind her. Charlie was still standing in the middle of the kitchen, looking frantic and anxious and . . . lost.

"Everything is *fine,* Charlie," she said swiftly. "Really. I'm having an off day; everyone has an off day sometimes. *Women.* Isn't that what you always say?"

"Sure." Charlie turned away from her, his hands in the cupboard. "You got his number?"

"Actually . . . that won't help," she said breezily. The breezy tone collapsed; she had the terrible feeling she was going to burst into tears again. Desperately, she smiled at him. "Listen, you think you can cope here?"

"Sure, I'll make the dinner—"

"Actually, I'm not really all that hungry. I—" She waved her hand, trying to explain without words, because suddenly she seemed to have an unbudgeable knot in her throat. "I'm going out for a while. Okay?"

It clearly wasn't okay with Charlie. "Listen—"

"Charlie, everything is *fine,*" she said once more.

"Okay, okay," he soothed.

She slipped out the back door. The last thing she wanted to do was upset Charlie, but there was no possible way she could handle being around anyone.

And blessedly there was no one to handle in the yard. The sun was low on the horizon, big and yellow. Belle started whinnying almost before Sonia opened the stable doors. Always, the mare had been sensitive to her mistress's scent. It took only a moment to saddle Belle, and all the while the mare was nuzzling Sonia's shoulder, clearly searching for the apple or sugar cube that wasn't there. "Sorry, sweetheart," Sonia murmured. "I'll bring you a treat later, Belle, if you'll promise to be good. Promise?"

She talked nonsense for a few more minutes, trying to soothe herself more than Belle. It didn't work. He'd been gone for four hours. By now he was in Chicago. It might as well have been a million miles away. Her heart was racing at just that many miles per hour, and there didn't seem to be a damn thing she could do to stop it. How could the hurt just keep on coming?

She was still wearing the violet jumpsuit and high-heeled sandals from her trip to town. She slipped off the sandals, stuck one bare foot into the stirrup, and vaulted onto Belle's back. The horse nickered responsively, as if able to sense her mood.

In a moment they were off at a brisk trot that turned into a canter and then a gallop. A hot wind streaked through Belle's mane and combed back Sonia's hair; they headed for the canyon road as if they shared the same fierce desire to be alone. Tears burned in Sonia's eyes, welcome in that loneliness.

Craig jammed on the brakes, sending a billow of dust out behind the car. Before he climbed out, he saw Charlie running out the back door as if demons were after him.

Craig didn't smile. Slamming the car door, he said abruptly, "Where is she?"

"I swear, you look worse than she does."

"Charlie—"

"She went off on that dang-fool mare up into the hills. I didn't know what the hell to do. I thought of going after her, but I—"

Craig waved the rest of the talk aside. He shrugged out of his suit jacket as he hit the kitchen, and had his shirt unbuttoned before he reached the hall. Less than five minutes later, he was dressed in jeans and riding boots.

Charlie met him halfway to the stable, Black Lightning's bridle in his hands. "I didn't take the time to saddle him," he said gruffly.

"Thanks, Charlie."

"You want I should—"

"No."

"Maybe you should just let her go. She was mighty upset."

Craig shot him a speaking look. Charlie abruptly subsided, plucked a cigar from his pocket, jammed it between his teeth, and headed for the house. "I knew you wouldn't go far, no matter what she thought," he muttered.

Craig barely heard. He'd spent four hours driving around. One wide sweep had taken him to the airport; after that, he wasn't sure what roads he'd taken or why.

He could have been in Chicago by now. No matter what Sonia thought, all he'd planned to do was contact an attorney, press charges, and seek retribution in a civilized way against their attacker. That was a rational plan, and all his life he'd been a rational man.

Emotionally—damn Sonia!—he'd had an image in his head from the minute the police called him. Just one punch in the man's face. *Something*. To get revenge . . .

But the plane had taken off without him. He'd just stood there, his ticket in hand, his anger surrounding him like an aura, a rage for which he had no outlet. Sonia . . . had known what was in his head, but she didn't understand. There was no possible way he could make her understand. She wasn't a man. It was that simple.

So was the sudden soul-wrenching fear of losing her. Just that simple.

His knees pressed into the horse's flanks and Black Lightning surged forward, knowing where they were going without being told. He had barely twenty minutes of daylight left. The wind ruffled through Black Lightning's mane, and in the pale light of dusk Craig's features took on a primitive cast, hard and austere, his eyes as hard as wet stones.

Fear was something he'd never had to deal with before. He hadn't been afraid in Chicago. But he was now.

Black Lightning strained for greater speed. The powerful animal's muscles surged beneath Craig's thighs in the rhythm of a race. He had to find her.

The colors from the setting sun painted the entire sky. Deep rose and amethyst glowed above the bleak, rocky landscape all around her. Not a rabbit stirred, not a bird. Sonia paused, stroking Belle's smooth neck. Both of them had slowed to an aimless walk.

There was nowhere to go. The huge western sky just kept on coming; the land offered no shelter...certainly not the kind of shelter that might have comforted her. Belle's flanks were damp; Sonia could feel a streak of dirt on her cheek. She was exhausted, weary from the fierce ride to nowhere and weary in her heart. Sand and dust had coated every inch of her skin, and she knew that all too soon the night would turn cold.

Once more she glanced toward home with despair in her eyes. Instead of total emptiness, though, she saw a cloud of dust coming toward her from the mouth of the canyon to the west. Her heart picked up the oddest fluttering pulse, and then she held her breath altogether. As she watched, the billowing dust took form.

Her heart suddenly soared sky-high. Still, it took several seconds for the faintest smile to form on her lips. Bending down, she whispered to Belle, as a sweet blur of tears filled her eyes. Happy tears.

Craig knew she'd seen him because he'd watched her head turn. Then she turned again and, with her long legs pressed to Belle's flanks, she bent low over the horse's mane and raced away from him. Where she thought she could run to he had no idea. And that she even wanted to run . . .

He dug his knees into Black Lightning's sides and bent low. The animal seemed to sense the desperate urgency in his master and burst forward in rollicking chase. They gained a hundred yards, and then another hundred. Minutes later Craig could see the shape of her legs pressed tightly against her horse, the wild, whipping curl of her hair. And then she switched directions and left a soaring cloud of dust behind her.

She made a mistake in doing that. A big mistake in judgment. He cut to her left, closing the distance by fifty yards, then another thirty. Both horse and rider increased their speed in one last burst of energy. In seconds, they were only a length behind her.

From nowhere, she raised both hands high in the air, balancing only with her legs on the horse. Horrified, Craig closed the last bit of distance between them, grappled an iron hand around her ribs, and snatched her free before she could fall. Belle's reins floated off as the mare continued the race into the distance, her load that much lighter.

He fought to slow his horse and at the same time kept a tight grip, very tight grip, on his wife. Black Lightning ground to a stop, his lungs heaving. Craig dropped the reins and pulled Sonia up from her precarious, and undoubtedly uncomfortable, position upside down across his thighs.

Wanting to shout at her for her damn-fool stunt, somehow he didn't. He tugged her close instead, wrapping his arms around her, winding her legs around his. For the first time in hours, he took a deep, relaxed breath. She was as dirty as a kid let loose in a sand pit. She still smelled like Sonia, whatever soap she used, whatever shampoo she used, whatever perfume she used. Whatever the hell was underneath all of that made such a difference.

For several minutes, he just held her, until he could work up a little rage again. That wasn't easy, when all he wanted was to love her and love her and love her... Finally, he reached up to tug at her hair. "Would you care to tell me what the hell you thought you were doing?"

He meant to sound furious; somehow his voice only sounded gravelly with emotion. He also meant for that little tug to punish just a little, but instead, his fingers ended up caressing her hair, smoothing it gently back from her temples. Her face lifted to his. He hadn't expected to see the dance of laughter on her lips. There were tears streaking down her cheeks; in the darkness they looked like jewels.

He kissed away one tear and then another.

"Craig, I was so afraid you weren't—"

He kissed her trembling mouth, then. "You don't get rid of a damn fool that easily, little one."

"You weren't a fool. I never thought that..." Joy was pulsing through her, and relief. She didn't know whether to laugh or cry. She seemed to be doing both. "I'm just so glad..."

He lifted her down, then swung off the horse himself. She walked into his arms, sliding her hands around his waist, crisscrossing them around his back as if she could impress the brand of him on her own skin. They were both hot, damp-hot, horse-hot, emotion-hot... and the suddenness of night falling brought a chill that only the touch of him dispelled.

"Sonia, I'm sorry. I never, never meant to hurt you..." His lips pressed into her hair. "Come here, you," he growled suddenly.

"I'm right here."

"Not close enough." His palms framed her face and forced her chin up. He claimed her mouth, hard, rough, insistent. By the time his lips lifted from hers, she felt a calm settling through her like riches. More than that, his arms swept around her, warm and tender, in a hug so heartfelt and precious that she knew he really was home again. "Now, are you going to tell me why the hell you pulled that damn fool stunt?" he murmured in her ear.

"So you could play hero. So you could swoop down out of the western sky and play the cowboy claiming his woman." She shifted in his arms, drawing her wrists up around his neck. There was a swift flash of disbelief and even anger in his eyes, but she pressed her finger to his lips before he could say anything. She hadn't been playing games. Her laughter died as well as her tears; vibrant emotions played on her face. "Would you listen for a minute?" she whispered.

"I'm listening."

"You were there. I *knew* you were there to catch me. And maybe it was a little foolish," she admitted softly, "but I had to tell you—I had to *show* you..." She took a breath, trying to make the words somehow fit right. "Men have such strange ideas about heroes," she said quietly. "Heroes aren't pirates, and you can't identify them by shining armor, and they never really slay dragons."

When he tried to speak again, she pressed her finger firmly on his mouth.

"Being a man has nothing to do with using your fists or playing macho scenes," she said firmly. "A real hero builds his life with strength and courage. He hurts, because he feels things so deeply. He's vulnerable, and *there's* a quality that men never have the sense to be proud of. And most of all," she added, "a hero is there for his lady when she needs him. You *were* there, and I knew you would be. Now, if I have to spell out any further exactly what you are to me—"

"Sonia..." He was silent for a minute, and then his thumb brushed another tear from beneath her eye. Just one this time. "But if you ever pull a trick like that again, I swear I'll..."

"I understand that," she said gravely, but the soft shine of humor suddenly erased any last hint of tears.

"I'm not joking."

"I know you're not." And she wasn't smiling. "You want to protect me, Craig? Then do it. I need that from you. I need to feel free to be vulnerable with you, to show you my weaker side, to feel free just to take the risks we need to take day by day to grow together. That's the kind of protection I need from you as a man, as *my* man, and I need it badly. It isn't a showy kind of thing; it's not as flamboyantly male as punching out some dude who looks at me sideways, or preventing me from falling off my horse."

"Dammit, I love you. Now, would you kindly shut up?" He tugged her close. "You can quit lecturing now," he growled in her ear, but his tone was loving.

"You're sure you've got it?"

"You talk more than any woman I've ever met in my entire life." The last image of the long-faced man with pale eyes dissolved in front of his eyes. Maybe that incident was always going to be more important to him than it was to her, but he now saw what an obsession he'd made of it. The woman in front of him filled his vision, a saucy shine to her eyes, a warmth and love radiating from her that cried out for him to swoop down for yet another kiss.

His lips found hers, coming home. She was trembling unaccountably. Sonia's front was partially bravado, the saucy shine in her eyes only half real. The longer his arms stayed around her, the longer his mouth stayed on hers, the closer he rubbed his body to hers, the more her trembling intensified.

Sonia was vulnerable. His male instinct to protect her was never going to die. He'd just had a few things mixed up. She wanted his love to protect her.

She had it. For a lifetime.

WONDERFUL ROMANCE NEWS!

Do you know about the exciting SECOND CHANCE AT LOVE/TO HAVE AND TO HOLD newsletter? Are you on our *free* mailing list? If reading all about your favorite authors, getting sneak previews of their latest releases, and being filled in on all the latest happenings and events in the romance world sound good to you, then you'll love our SECOND CHANCE AT LOVE and TO HAVE AND TO HOLD Romance News.

If you'd like to be added to our mailing list, just fill out the coupon below and send it in...and we'll send you your *free* newsletter every three months — hot off the press.

☐ *Yes, I would like to receive your free SECOND CHANCE AT LOVE/TO HAVE AND TO HOLD newsletter.*

Name _____

Address _____

City _____ **State/Zip** _____

Please return this coupon to:

Berkley Publishing
200 Madison Avenue, New York, New York 10016
Att: Rebecca Kaufman

HERE'S WHAT READERS ARE SAYING ABOUT

To Have and to Hold™

"Your TO HAVE AND TO HOLD series is a fabulous and long overdue idea."
—*A. D., Upper Darby, PA**

"I have been reading romance novels for over ten years and feel the TO HAVE AND TO HOLD series is the best I have read. It's exciting, sensitive, refreshing, well written. Many thanks for a series of books I can relate to."
—*O. K., Bensalem, PA**

"I enjoy your books tremendously."
—*J. C., Houston, TX**

"I love the books and read them over and over."
—*E. K., Warren, MI**

"You have another winner with the new TO HAVE AND TO HOLD series."
—*R. P., Lincoln Park, MI**

"I love the new series TO HAVE AND TO HOLD."
—*M. L., Cleveland, OH**

"I've never written a fan letter before, but TO HAVE AND TO HOLD is fantastic."
—*E. S., Narberth, PA**

*Name and address available upon request

Second Chance at Love®